IT WAS A BLISS THAT KEPT CLIMBING HIGHER AND HIGHER . . .

Her arms tightened around him, her fingers buried themselves in his hair at the base of his neck. His lips demanded more of her.

He swept her on and on in the newfound world of ecstasy until finally all that existed were fiery lights, the fire and the shuddering transporting her into a whirling land of sensation beyond description. It seemed she would never catch her breath. . . .

CANDLELIGHT ECSTASY ROMANCES™

38 SUMMER STORMS, *Stephanie St. Clair*
39 WINTER WINDS, *Jackie Black*
40 CALL IT LOVE, *Ginger Chambers*
41 THE TENDER MENDING, *Lia Sanders*
42 THE ARDENT PROTECTOR, *Bonnie Drake*
43 A DREAM COME TRUE, *Elaine Raco Chase*
44 NEVER AS STRANGERS, *Suzanne Simmons*
45 RELENTLESS ADVERSARY, *Jayne Castle*
46 RESTORING LOVE, *Suzanne Sherrill*
47 DAWNING OF DESIRE, *Susan Chatfield*
48 MASQUERADE OF LOVE, *Alice Morgan*
49 ELOQUENT SILENCE, *Rachel Ryan*
50 SNOWBOUND WEEKEND, *Amii Lorin*
51 ALL'S FAIR, *Anne N. Reisser*
52 REMEMBRANCE OF LOVE, *Cathie Linz*
53 A QUESTION OF TRUST, *Dorothy Ann Bernard*
54 SANDS OF MALIBU, *Alice Morgan*
55 AFFAIR OF RISK, *Jayne Castle*
56 DOUBLE OCCUPANCY, *Elaine Raco Chase*
57 BITTER VINES, *Megan Lane*
58 WHITE WATER LOVE, *Alyssa Morgan*
59 A TREASURE WORTH SEEKING, *Rachel Ryan*
60 LOVE, YESTERDAY AND FOREVER, *Elise Randolph*
61 LOVE'S WINE, *Frances Flores*
62 TO LOVE A STRANGER, *Hayton Monteith*
63 THE METAL MISTRESS, *Barbara Cameron*
64 SWEET HEALING PASSION, *Samantha Scott*
65 HERITAGE OF THE HEART, *Nina Pykare*
66 DEVIL'S PLAYGROUND, *JoAnna Brandon*
67 IMPETUOUS SURROGATE, *Alice Morgan*
68 A NEGOTIATED SURRENDER, *Jayne Castle*
69 STRICTLY BUSINESS, *Gloria Renwick*
70 WHISPERED PROMISE, *Bonnie Drake*
71 MARRIAGE TO A STRANGER, *Dorothy Phillips*
72 DESIGNING WOMAN, *Elaine Raco Chase*
73 A SPARK OF FIRE IN THE NIGHT, *Elise Randolph*
74 CAPTIVE DESIRE, *Tate McKenna*
75 CHAMPAGNE AND RED ROSES, *Sheila Paulos*
76 COME LOVE, CALL MY NAME, *Anne N. Reisser*
77 MASK OF PASSION, *Kay Hooper*

TO CATCH THE WILD WIND

Jo Calloway

A CANDLELIGHT ECSTASY ROMANCE™

Published by
Dell Publishing Co., Inc.
1 Dag Hammarskjold Plaza
New York, New York 10017

Dell ® TM 681510, Dell Publishing Co., Inc.

Candlelight Ecstasy Romance™ is a trademark of
Dell Publishing Co., Inc., New York, New York.

ISBN 0-440-11126-9

Printed in the United States of America
First printing—September 1982

To Our Readers:

We have been delighted with your enthusiastic response to Candlelight Ecstasy Romances™ and we thank you for the interest you have shown in this exciting series.

In the upcoming months, we will continue to present the distinctive, sensuous love stories you have come to expect only from Ecstasy. We look forward to bringing you many more books from your favorite authors and also, the very finest work from new authors of contemporary romantic fiction.

As always, we are striving to present the unique, absorbing love stories that you enjoy most—books that are more than ordinary romance.

Your suggestions and comments are always welcome. Please write to us at the address below.

Sincerely,

The Editors
Candlelight Romances
1 Dag Hammarskjold Plaza
New York, N.Y. 10017

TO CATCH
THE WILD WIND

CHAPTER ONE

Kicking the silvery foliage from around her bare ankles, Kenda Vaughn made her way slowly through the dark, glossy, green forest. She was oblivious to the enchanting scene that surrounded her, focusing her attention only upon the potatolike roots she held in her hands. She ignored the tall forms of the coconut palms that moved their graceful plumes high above her head and paid no attention to the monkeys playing nearby, swinging noisily from tree to tree. Beautiful, bright-colored birds flitted from the pale green trees to nest in the tremendous banyan—a tree that looked like a forest within itself, but in reality was only a single tree with dozens of branches that had taken root and become a tree within a tree.

Not even the banyan interested her anymore. The wonderful peculiarity of downward-growing branches had long since become ordinary to her. She had been sixteen when she first examined the tree with the light-colored

11

bark and the strange branches that hung down, took root, and became covered with bark like the parent stem. No change of expression crossed her face now as she glimpsed the tree with its noisy inhabitants, then walked on.

For years she had hoped against hope that someone—anyone—would come to the island and find her. She had cried and prayed and suffered a loneliness she felt would destroy her if she had to be confined in this place for the remainder of her life. But that had been almost seven years ago, and over the years her tears had dried, her prayers had ceased, her loneliness had changed to a quiet feeling of contentment. She was sure now that she would never be found and she had long ago begun to think of this isolated tropical island as the only home she would ever again have on earth.

She could hardly remember what life had been like before that sixteenth summer of her life when she sailed away from the harbor in San Francisco to spend her summer vacation with her father at his island laboratory. He had met her on the South Pacific island of Suva, the main Fiji Island. From Suva, a half day's flight by helicopter, they had traveled to the laboratory. During the flight her father had explained to her that the island was almost completely inaccessible by boat.

There had only been two other people on the small uninhabited island with him to assist in his work as chief research biologist of the Institute of Marine Life, and they, along with her father, had perished in the sudden tropical storm that burst upon the island in the middle of what had begun as a bright, sunny afternoon. She had been in the forest that day, gathering the golden fruit from the bread-fruit trees and had not seen the dark clouds blow in without warning from the howling sea. When she realized the force of the wind that caught and bent the trees almost to the ground, she panicked. Fighting against the wind's fury, she tried to make her way back to the open shoreline settlement and to her father, but she did not. The wind, splitting off a branch from a large tree, blew it downward to strike her across the skull, sending her into an immediate state of total unconsciousness and burying her beneath a layer of brush and leaves.

Over the days that followed she could remember fleeting hints of a returning alertness; she could remember opening her eyes to see a pretty parakeet with a green body and bright red breast on a branch above her. She heard it chirping before unconsciousness again snatched her away. At intervals she could hear monkeys squealing and chattering in the high branches overhead.

She had no idea how long she lay on the nature-cushioned ground, weaving in and out of consciousness, but it was the most tragic day of her young life when she awoke to full consciousness and rose slowly on weakened limbs. Stumbling and crawling, she fought her way back to the coast. Although it had only taken a matter of minutes for her usually strong legs to carry her into the forest, it now took hours for her to wend her way out of the heavy growth of trees and plants. Fatigued and frightened, but hanging on with a strength from some unknown source, she fought a growing terror. When the coast finally broke into her view in the fading light of evening, a horror she had never dreamed of met her youthful eyes. Her heart slowed, then stopped completely. There was nothing left. Silent and deserted was the high strip of land where the laboratory and the thatched-roof bungalows had stood.

Nothing but a few bricks from the chimney and a few scattered planks from the two buildings lay on the sand. With dull eyes Kenda stared dumbly at the nothingness before unconsciousness descended on her again and wiped the ugly picture from her eyes.

In the days that followed Kenda sat close by the sea and waited. She wept and screamed and pleaded to the heavens for help to come. The days she existed in the uttermost depths of grief and horror went by uncounted. Then one day she realized that help would not be coming. It dawned on her that help had already been to the island. That was why there were no corpses, no equipment scattered in the sand. She had lain unconscious when the helicopter swept in from the large island, collected the bodies and equipment, and then flew away again. Help had been to the island already, and she had been left for dead.

Still, for weeks she hoped against hope that she would look out and see a ship approaching on the horizon. But soon all hope died, her heart sank deep within her chest, and she turned her remaining dismal thoughts to survival. That night she made herself a bed of ferns in the shelter of an overhanging rock and covered herself with a quilt of dried, stretched moss, interwoven with vines and leaves. Looking out in the dark at the white waves that lashed the reefs and shore, she knew that only a miracle would bring a ship the hundred and fifty miles from the well-traveled ocean paths that connected the main islands to this remote paradise that lay almost completely encapsulated by reefs of coral. With that bleak thought in mind she fell asleep.

Sometimes she would dream that another biologist would want to continue her father's work and come to rebuild the laboratory research center on the island. She liked to dream that dream, but after several years, that dream, too, vanished from her mind.

She grew tall and strong and healthy. Food was plentiful all around her. The valley beyond the forest on the other side of the island grew wild vegetables, large yams, and the long potatolike roots that she harvested every few days. She had plums, bananas, coconuts, breadfruit, and chestnuts from the trees that grew along the freshwater stream. Some days she would eat continuously and drink water and coconut milk; other days she would not touch a bite of food, but would only drink the clear water from the stream that flowed into a placid-surfaced lake in the valley. In that lake of clear blue water she could see her reflection. The lake became her mirror and she watched herself change from a frail, terrified sixteen-year-old into a bronze-skinned, firm woman with long sun-bleached hair the color of the morning sun. Her eyes were the color of the lagoon water, a clear sparkling gray-blue surrounded by long black lashes. Most of the time she wore no clothing, having but the two garments she had worn from the cottage that day of the storm. She had kept the material of the torn cotton blouse and jeans, pulling the seams out thread by thread and with a quill-like needle had sewn the material into a single garment she could loop around her body to cover her nakedness. Rarely did she use the garment.

She slept during the dark hours of night in the vine-covered hut she had built with her bare hands of branches held together by ropes of vine. The hut was built around the overhanging ledge where she slept. With the bricks and wooden boards she had constructed two tables. One was her dinner table, the other held the remnants of several books that had belonged to her father, which she had found days after the storm, scattered in the foliage at the edge of the forest. Her collection consisted of parts of a dictionary, two books on marine biology with only a few pages missing from each, a book on shells intact except for the front and back covers, and various paperback adventures, titles unknown. Every day she read. She would sit in the afternoons at the edge of the forest and read aloud. Most days creatures from the jungle would gather nearby with watchful eyes and listen to the sound of her voice. Almost seven years had lapsed from that first day she picked up a book and proceeded to speak the words aloud. Civilization was not completely dead to her.

Stealthily she moved through the flowered growth, breathing in the air heavy with the sweet, perfumed scent. Her taste buds craved the potato roots she held in her hands. As she walked out of the dense black-green, she smiled to herself, thinking of her soon-to-be luscious meal. She headed for the hut. Suddenly she wheeled to her left and dropped the roots in the sand. There, not more than two hundred yards away in the lagoon, a beautiful sailboat lay anchored.

For an instant she could not believe her eyes. Her mouth dropped open and she stood helpless, not knowing what to do. A short scream escaped her throat when a voice behind her boomed out: "My God in heaven! Wha-what are you doing here!"

She did not immediately turn around to see the origin of the startling sound. Petrified, the only sounds heard were her astonished gasps.

16

When at last she could move again, she cut a hurried glance over her shoulder in the direction of the voice. Directly behind her, in open-mouthed disbelief, stood a man.

CHAPTER TWO

Quickly Kenda dashed into the hut, seconds later reappearing, the short, faded tunic wrapped around her body.

"Who are you?" the man called out to her in a still very much alarmed voice. "What in heaven's name are you doing here? Are you alone?"

Kenda, as bewildered as he, stood speechless a few steps from the hut. She looked at him with wide eyes. She had not expected this to happen, and now that it had, she found herself disastrously unprepared. She watched the tall, handsome man with pouting lips and dark brown eyes, a mass of windblown auburn curls tangled across his forehead. He wore shorts and T-shirt that revealed a body of firm muscles. She tried to open her mouth and speak to him, but she could not.

"Tell me"—his voice was much softer, his shock seemed to be fading—"who are you? What are you doing here?" He began to walk toward her. "Can you speak?"

Backing away, she licked her lips. "I . . . I . . . my name is Kenda . . . Kenda Vaughn." She had finally gotten past her mute barrier. "Kenda . . . Vaughn," she repeated, not removing her eyes from him. Fear registered clear on her face.

He was close to her now. "Kenda." He nodded, then continued with patience. "Tell me, what are you doing on this island? Are you alone?"

"I—I have been here a long time. I came here to visit my father when I was sixteen."

"Where is your father?"

"He—he died in a storm. Two other men died with him. I never could find them after the storm. I know he died or he would have come back for me."

"Vaughn." He let a silence fall while he stared at her. After a while, he repeated, "Vaughn . . . Harold Vaughn, the marine biologist?"

Kenda nodded wildly. "Yes, yes. That was my father."

"My God!" he exclaimed. "That must have been almost seven years ago. You've been here all this time by yourself?" He came closer, the disbelief contorting his tanned face.

Kenda nodded and her lips trembled.

With a strange and sudden tenderness he leaned forward, bent his head, and brushed her lips with his. When she swayed, he reached out and caught her, pulling her close to his body. He whispered into her ear, "I'm sorry. I just couldn't help myself. You can't imagine how beautiful you are."

Startled, she drew apart from him and said, "You shouldn't have done that." Her innocent eyes fastened on his as she touched her lips with her fingertips.

He laughed and shook his head. "No." He took a step backward and held up both hands. "No, I shouldn't have. I'm sorry." Again he laughed, this time uneasily.

She watched him laugh, then asked solemnly, "Who are you? Where did you come from?"

"John." He continued to smile. "John Taylor. I live in Los Angeles. Do you remember where Los Angeles is?"

Kenda nodded. "Yes. In California. We lived there when I was small."

"Where was your last home, Kenda?"

"Honolulu. That's where we lived just before I came here."

"Do you have a family in Honolulu, a mother . . . brothers . . . sisters?"

Kenda shook her head. "There was only my father and me. We had a housekeeper named Leah."

Rubbing his chin thoughtfully, John Taylor began to walk away from her. "I see," he said almost inaudibly.

Kenda began to walk after him. "How did you get here? The reefs are very dangerous, did you not know?" Her voice sounded strange to her own ears. Talking with someone was not at all like reading aloud.

He stopped and faced her. "I guess you could say my adventurous spirit brought me here. I sailed near here three summers ago, but I wasn't brave enough to venture past the reefs." He shrugged. "Why this year, I don't know. Maybe I'm a better sailor, or perhaps I have more self-confidence. Who knows? Anyway, the water's clear enough so that all the reefs are visible. I just hope it stays that way."

Kenda offered her first fleeting smile. "I'm glad you

came. I didn't think anyone would ever come. I had given up hope."

John Taylor gave a good-natured laugh. "Never give up, that's the first Taylor rule. If anything out of the ordinary is going to happen, I'll guarantee you John Taylor will not be far off." He started walking again toward the small dinghy on the sand. "How many men do you suppose dream of sailing off into the blue and coming upon some remote tropical island in the bright sunshine and finding a beautiful maiden among the coconut palms?" He stopped and raised his brows at her. "But how many actually do?" He held up one finger. "One. John Taylor."

She looked puzzled. "Are you not happy you found me?"

"I doubt that *happy* is the right word. In any event, I have found you, so the question is what will I do with you now that I have."

Kenda's blue eyes widened before the corners of her mouth dropped.

"Don't look so disappointed," he said softly. "I'm not going to leave you here." He continued toward the dinghy. "I've just got to think. You've caught me a bit by surprise." Reaching the dinghy, he pulled it forward onto the sand until it was completely out of the water. Looking back at her, he said, "Let me think."

"What is there to think? You will take me on your boat. What is there to think?" She found him surveying her with a half-mocking smile on her lips.

"Indeed," he paused, shrugging. "You make it sound very simple. Just load you on board and the two of us sail off into the sunset. What then? Where do we go after we've gone past the sunset? Do I take you to an island and turn you over to American officials? Is that what I do with you?"

"Oh, no. No!"

"What's wrong with that? You'll be taken care of. Heavens, Kenda, I can't be responsible for you. I don't have the time."

She forced herself to look unflinchingly into his dark brown eyes. She could sense now that the initial shock was over and he did not seem happy to have found her on the island. His eyes had a curiously disturbing glare in them.

"Don't look at me that way," he commanded, eyes suddenly flashing. "I didn't say that was what I'd do, but it's certainly worthy of thought. At any rate, we'll do what's best for you."

With a pleading look, Kenda said, "I would rather stay with you."

John said nothing. He loudly cleared his throat and looked at the thirty-foot ketch anchored in the cove. He stood motionless, eyeing the boat. After a while, he said, "Why don't we round up something to eat? I'm starving."

Kenda silently spun around and began kicking at the sand, looking down at her feet. She hesitated, then ran a few steps toward the hut, stopped again, and scanned the sand.

After watching her a minute, John blurted out, "What in the hell are you doing?"

"My roots. I dropped my potato roots."

"I'm not eating any potato roots!"

The meal was prepared outside the hut in the shifting lights of a dull, ominous sunset. Kenda had brought her table outside and scrubbed the boards with seawater before placing the bananas, coconuts, and potato roots on it. She looked up at the sky now and studied it before turning her attention to the dinghy coming ashore from the boat. She pondered. If she told John a storm was approaching, he might try to sail away in the fading light and that would be most terrible for them both. There would be no way to get past the reefs in the darkness.

He pulled the small boat from the water and Kenda noticed he carried a canvas bag in his hand as he walked toward her. He had changed his clothes. He wore denims, a plaid shirt, sneakers, and socks, and his curly reddish brown hair had been combed. She smiled up at him from where she sat in the sand beside the table.

"Here." He held out the bag to her. "My contribution to supper and . . . uh . . . there are some clothes inside for you to put on." He sat down across from her and watched her with a half-anxious smile as she lifted a package of crackers, a can of tuna, two Cokes, and two small cans of vanilla pudding from inside the canvas. Next she lifted out a navy pullover shirt and a pair of faded denims. At the bottom waited a pair of deck shoes and socks.

"You want me to put these on now?"

"If you don't mind." He reached for the can of tuna and removed an all-purpose knife from his pocket. "I'll open this while you change."

Slowly she got to her feet. Impulsively she pulled the front of the tunic. "I made this," she said in little above a whisper. "You don't like it, do you?"

He smiled and white teeth sparkled in the dusk. "Oh, I like it. I—uh—I like it very much. It's just that I would feel more comfortable if you had just a bit more on, you know."

Kenda stood motionless, waiting. After a moment, she asked, "I know?"

John looked at her questioningly. "What is it?"

"You said 'I know.' What is it I know?"

Hurriedly he finished opening the can and placed it on the table. Without meeting her eyes, he said, "You know about men and women, don't you, Kenda? You know about how—" He paused awkwardly. "About how men and women—uh—sometimes have relationships."

"Yes," she replied adamantly. "I most certainly do. I am not a child, John Vaughn. I knew all about sex when I was eight years old."

"Well, darling, as knowledgeable as you apparently are, you must have forgotten something, otherwise you wouldn't be in the company of a grown man who hasn't been with a woman in months wearing just that thing wrapped around you."

Tucking the clothes under her arm, she walked briskly into the hut. Fighting back the tears, she dressed in his clothes, then walked back outside and looked at him shyly. "Is this better?"

"Much." He motioned her to sit down. "Let's eat." He lit a lantern he'd brought to shore and placed it in the middle of the table. Then he lifted a hunk of tuna from the can and placed it on a cracker. Putting the whole thing in his mouth, he chewed and watched her.

Carefully she lifted the Coke to her mouth and took a small sip. She swallowed. For a moment her face was totally emotionless, then she burst out laughing. "I have not tasted a Coke in so long." She laughed again. "It tickles my throat, like swallowing bubbles."

"That's because it's warm," he said matter-of-factly. His gaze slowly swept her face—her golden hair was caught in the web of lantern light and fell softly to her knees—then came to rest on the unusually large, pale blue eyes that watched him unblinkingly. He wore a strange, humorless smile.

Reluctantly she lifted the Coke again, took a drink, but this time when she swallowed she did not laugh. She was beginning to feel herself flush painfully under his watchful eyes. She knew she wasn't a young girl, but his expression made her feel like one. She reached for a cracker and gave him a quick discreet smile. "Aren't you hungry?" she asked, noticing he had stopped eating.

Ignoring her question, John spoke in a subdued voice. "I suppose we'll leave in the morning with the tide."

Kenda considered whether or not to tell him about the storm. Again she dissuaded herself from doing so.

He stretched, lifting his arms high above his head. "Ummm." He looked at Kenda. "I'm sleepy. Guess I'll go back to the *Beauty* and get a good night's rest."

"*Beauty?* Is that your boat's name?"

He nodded, starting to rise.

"Isn't that an unusual name for a boat? I thought *Beauty* was a horse's name. Why did you name your boat that?"

A silence fell and he settled back on the sand. "I didn't name her."

"Who named her?"

"A child," he said quietly, and torment leaped into his eyes before he could hide it. "My little girl named her."

Kenda felt a chill steal over her at this unexpected

revelation. Suddenly it dawned on her that she knew nothing about the man sitting across from her. If he had a child, then he also had a wife. And if he had a wife and a child, why was he sailing alone? Where were they? But she would not be allowed any more questions. He was on his feet again. "Must you go now?"

"Yes."

She sat, watching him walk to the dinghy, climb in, then row out to the *Beauty*. The loneliness she experienced at that moment was like the loneliness she had experienced years ago when she awoke to find herself alone on the island. She yearned to be with him, to talk with him, to hear his voice. She sighed. She knew she probably sounded foolish to him. Foolish and boring. She had been a fool to expect that she might converse with someone after all these years and even sound half sensible. She had bored him and he had left her without even eating his supper. She saw the light go out in the cabin and her heart dropped even farther into her chest as she sighed again.

A stiff breeze blew inland and lifted her hair from her face, carrying it backward over her shoulders. With the cool air sweeping her body, she was still conscious of a warmth rising in her, a feeling she had never before felt, something she could not name.

CHAPTER THREE

Kenda tossed and turned on her bed of ferns as the low rumble of thunder filled her ears. Her mind wound back across the years. She had thought that to leave the island was the greatest of her wishes, and now that the time was actually close, to her surprise she felt a sadness. Even in the wake of the approaching storm she could smell the soft, sweet fragrances that surrounded her. She allowed her thoughts to ramble, mentally tracing her paths through the trees and shrubs to the low green valley and back again. The storm outside did not frighten her, but the feelings inside her filled her with a fear. She began thinking perplexing and devastating thoughts. What if she left her island to find herself never again content or happy? She remembered the expression of delight on John Taylor's face when he first saw her, then the unfathomable one he wore when he walked away from her. She thought of his lips brushing hers. It had not been a real kiss. Al Upton had given her a real kiss the night he brought her home from the school dance when she was thirteen. She felt he would mash all her teeth out, but Al's real kiss, and all the other boys she had kissed, had done nothing but leave her with bruised lips, while John Taylor's mere touch had melted the substance in her knees and left her puzzled.

She heard the ocean wind blow fiercely onto the island. Quickly she hopped from her bed, ran to the doorway of the hut, and pulled apart the curtain of plumes that was secured at the top by heavy vines. She looked straight out into John Taylor's face.

"Lady," he said, "that is a wild wind out there." He cut worried glances to the cove where his boat thrashed about in the turbulent surf.

Pulling the plumes together in his face, Kenda ran quickly across the room to where her new clothes lay in a neat stack. She dressed in less than a second and turned back to the doorway. He stood inside, holding a flashlight at his side, staring at her.

While a storm raged outside the hut a silence enveloped them in the swaying structure. Kenda looked at John desperately, as if to say "please like me."

"Do you think we're safe here?" he finally asked.

She nodded. "Yes. The worst has passed." Magically the wind seemed to die away with her words.

The water ran along the lines of his face from his hair, which had been blown around his forehead, and being wet had plastered to his skin. He reached up and wiped his face with his hand. "I'm afraid the wind damaged my main mast. I won't really be able to tell until daybreak. I know my sail and rigging is in the water." He shook his head. "I had no idea a storm was brewing. I guess I'll need to pay closer attention to weather bulletins."

Kenda winced with guilt. "I—I knew about the storm," she admitted, bracing herself against the ledge.

"You what?" Disbelief sounded in his voice and his dark eyes narrowed at her. "How?"

Her voice heavy as stone she said, "I could tell by the clouds."

"Why didn't you tell me, Kenda?"

"I was afraid you would try to leave."

"I would have, but I would have taken you with me. Is that what you feared, that I would leave you here on the island?"

Kenda shook her head. "No. We would have wrecked on the reefs."

His sudden stillness made her more restless than an open display of anger would have.

"You don't think much of my sailing ability, do you?" he said after a long pause.

"Oh, no, John, that isn't it. I promise. It's just that nobody can sail past those reefs in the dark." She made herself smile at him. "I'm sure you're a very good sailor or you wouldn't be here in the first place."

"Oh, well, it's not important. At any rate, it's doubtful we'll be able to catch the morning tide. It's doubtful we'll be able to leave at all today." Ducking his head, he started out the opening.

She took a step toward him. "John?"

He looked back. "What is it?"

"Please don't go." She motioned him back inside and pointed to the table where bananas and coconuts lay untouched from the earlier meal. "There's food. Please stay and talk to me."

"All right," he said, stepping back inside. He sat down on the packed-sand floor beside the table and reached for a banana. "But only for a few minutes."

She fell on her knees across from him, her eyes dancing. "Tell me about your little girl."

His jaws clamped together hard. Without a word he took out his knife and slit holes in the coconut, then drank down a large swallow of the milk. "I'd rather not, Kenda," he said flatly after swallowing.

She just sat staring at him.

"Why don't we talk about you?" he said after a few minutes of silence.

She liked the way he said that. His tone was suddenly light and pleasant. "What about me? There's nothing to tell about me."

He dropped the banana peel and folded his hands on the table. He grinned. "Well, miss, that may be what you think, but I'll guarantee you that there are many people in this world that won't quite believe it. Why, the very fact that you're alive is some kind of miracle. Don't you realize that? Kenda, you have survived the elements for somewhere in the vicinity of seven years. I may be wrong, but I believe when you return home you will become a celebrity of sorts. I'll be very surprised if you don't."

Her eyes widened. "Don't you see it hasn't been hard to stay alive. In the beginning I didn't know if I could keep my mind I was so messed up." She pulled her hair back from the left side of her face and showed him a scar that traveled a hidden path on her scalp to full view above her temporal area. "I can vaguely remember wandering around for days, maybe weeks, living on fruits and nuts I could reach, until finally I regained my strength, and my mind began to clear. I knew I'd been left for dead and for a while it seemed I would die." A sad little smile played along her lips. "Then I became healthy again and I knew I wouldn't die. For a while I didn't know which was worse: to die alone or to live alone." She finished and her smile disappeared.

John took a cigarette from his shirt pocket and lit it, avoiding eye contact with her. Shining the flashlight on the table of books, he asked, "Have those been your company?"

A smile reappeared, brighter than before. "Yes." She looked around at the row of old, fading books lined neatly on the table. "I have read them all dozens of times."

He smiled. "Even the dictionary?" He raised his brows at her.

She nodded with a laugh. "Even the dictionary. Several years ago I decided to memorize all the definitions. I made it through the M's before I realized I was quickly forgetting what was back in the A's. From then on I didn't try to remember all the definitions, just those words I found to be most interesting."

John stretched his legs out beside the table and his foot touched her leg. "Sorry," he muttered, drawing his legs back to their original position. "Tell me"—his voice sounded strained—"what do you remember about home?"

A faraway look crossed the light blue irises. "I remember it." Her voice grew soft, almost reverent. "Daddy bought a condominium for us. It was small and compact with just three bedrooms. Mine had pastel green walls and was trimmed in yellow. Downstairs was the living room and kitchen. Leah, our housekeeper, kept everything spotless. On my sixteenth birthday Father bought me a car—a dark blue Mustang." She shook her head. "I didn't get to drive it but a time or two." Suddenly she paused. "John, why did you apologize for touching my leg?"

He seemed to hesitate before saying, "I don't think it would be smart of either of us to encourage body contact, however slight or unintentional, Kenda." His tan face flushed. "It would not be wise, believe me."

"I don't mind."

John shook his head in amused exasperation. "You don't mind." He looked momentarily troubled. "Kenda, I doubt that you realize what a truly beautiful girl you are. If we allow ourselves to touch, or brush, or—anyway the point I'm trying to make is that something could happen between us that I don't want to happen, and I'm sure you aren't ready to have happen." He crushed out the cigarette, picked up a banana, and slid the peel halfway down.

"I'm not a child, John. My childhood was years ago. Look at me. I'm twenty-three years old, maybe older. What month is this?"

"April."

"Last month I was twenty-three. March twelfth. You see, I know what it was like to be young. I recall those days vividly. The mystery is that I don't know what it's like to be grown—and I am grown." She bit her lip. "I want to be grown-up with you, John." She pressed her hand tightly around his wrist. "I want you—"

Interrupting harshly he said, "Kenda, you must stop this." Freeing his arm from her grasp, he forced himself to his feet. "I must get back to the *Beauty*. As soon as it's

34

light I'll start to work on the damage done by the storm. Who knows how long it will take."

When he walked out without another word, Kenda was sickened with the disappointment of the moment. She wanted to rush out and follow his footsteps in the sand, to fling her arms around his body, to make him hold her in his arms. Seized by an overpowering restlessness, she clenched her hands together tightly as an invisible restraint to prevent her from running after him. Whatever the hunger was in her, it was growing.

After a while she walked outside the hut and breathed in a long breath of damp air. She walked across the sand to the edge of the forest where the shadows of the palms and chestnuts were faint on the sand, having just come to life in the weak glow of the moon which had been freed from the dark prison of clouds. She could hear the brisk lapping of the sea on the reefs behind. From a distance deep within the growth of trees the screams of parrots and the loud chatter of monkeys emerged. These were the sights and sounds to which she had become accustomed. Before yesterday there had been no other. Now there was the sound of her own thundering heartbeat and, even with her eyes closed, the sight of a man to join with all the other sights and sounds of her life. She sighed and calmly turned her eyes to the lagoon. The *Beauty* was dark.

In early morning light Kenda found John busily working on the mast, sails, and rigging. His back was to the white stretch of sandy beach. It was a beautiful, clear morning; the blue cloudless sky seemed never to have known a storm. The sunrise came with a bright burst of yellow on the horizon.

Keeping an eye on the boat, Kenda walked along the water's edge wearing the large blue pullover and jeans which she had rolled up to her knees. Her feet were bare and occasionally she would grip the sand between her toes, raise her foot, spread apart her toes and let the sand fall back onto the beach. She waited for John to turn around and shout a greeting or wave to her or do something to at least acknowledge that he was aware of her presence.

Part of her mind contemplated swimming out to the boat and climbing on board behind him, and the other part cautioned her against it. When he stood, she felt her heart jump, but it fell and she inclined her head when he sat down again without as much as a glance over his shoulder.

She felt tears in her eyes. Then she lifted her head proudly. "John Taylor," she said aloud, but still in a whisper, "if you don't want me with you, I won't go." Quickly she spun around and fled into the forest, not stopping to pause until she reached her valley.

The remainder of the morning and on into the afternoon passed like a bad dream. She could not understand what was happening to her. She bathed in the warm water of the lake, dressed, and spread out like a corpse on the soft grass with her eyes opened wide and fixed on the blue above her. She was thinking that she would let him sail away, just like he sailed in—unnoticed. Who would miss her if she never went back? Nobody. She had been dead to the world for almost seven years. Who would rejoice to know that she was alive? Did he? Still, deep down, she wanted to go back. She wanted to go back with him.

The day wore on and the wrangle in her mind continued. Sunset came in a brilliant burning gold, the light

36

drifting past her into the trees. Suddenly she heard a loud voice.

"Kenda!" it shouted.

She did not move.

It came again. "Kenda, where are you?"

She remained silent, but her mind spun wildly.

It did not come again. All was silent.

When she looked around and saw him, her eyes widened, but she made no attempt to speak.

His eyes glared at her. "If you don't mind, I'd like to ask what the hell you think you're doing? Where have you been all day?" Standing with his hands planted firmly on the sides of his hips, his feet braced apart, he raved on. "I could have used your help several times today, but where were you? Down here living the life of Riley. Well, I can tell you this, if you're going to sail with me, you can then expect to work with me."

She drew herself up into a sitting position. Sliding her arms around her legs, she rested her head on her knees and frowned. "I am not going with you," she said in slow deliberate words. "You don't want me with you. I won't go with you."

He looked at her with surprise and walked in silence to where she sat. He looked straight down at her, the sunlight tinting his eyes a golden brown. "Yes, Kenda, you will go with me. Fate has set you in my path, and you will go with me."

Her chin went up and she looked at him puzzled. "Fate?"

He knelt and they were face-to-face. "Yes, that mysterious lady—fate. Sometimes I think she picks on me." He hesitated. "Four years ago, the year I bought *Beauty,* I

37

had intended to take off a year and with my family I had planned to spend that time sailing these islands. I did take off a year and I did sail these islands, but alone. Then for some unexplainable reason, when I returned home, the thought of this island stuck in my head. I didn't think too often about the ones I sailed and explored, but I thought often of this one. So you see, fortunately, or perhaps unfortunately for you, fate brought me to this island and fate will take the two of us from here." He smiled a strange little smile and rose to his feet.

Kenda looked squarely at him and the daring of her own thoughts frightened her. She doubted there lived a more handsome man than John Taylor anywhere in the world. He was the tallest man she had ever known, lean and sinewy like a mountain lion. She studied his handsome face intently, searching for the slightest hint of a struggle hidden inside him as was inside her. He would not allow her search to be a long one, for quickly he turned back to the trees.

"Come on," he said, and motioned her to get up. "It's almost dark."

She forced her eyes to the darkening jungle that bordered the circular valley. In silence she climbed to her feet and walked easily toward the wall of intricate vines and trees. Now and again she would glance over her shoulder to make sure John followed close by. The foliage had thinned along the well-worn path, but in darkness all the greens seemed to blend together in an impregnable maze. She found it a pleasure to have John dependent on her, for she knew without her he would spend the night lost in the heavy growth. She walked on. It was a nice feeling.

"Is that thing a banyan tree?" he asked.

38

"Yes," she said knowingly. Already the green-black had thinned out. She pushed aside a long, leafy vine and felt the cool breeze of the sea on her face.

"I thought it was found only in India."

"No. Banyans are on many of the islands." Her words drifted backward to meet him. "My father told me that the tree has a religious significance to the people of India, but here it is only another tree."

Together they walked on to the beach. She looked out to the boat. "Is she ready?"

"No." He paused, then added, "I might have finished, but I didn't know what had happened to you, so I stopped working and started looking."

A devilish smile covered her lips. For her that seemed something of a victory.

Suddenly he snapped his fingers. "I have an idea," he said cheerfully. "Why don't we cook supper. A feast. I have a couple of fish that were caught up in the sails. We'll cook them. How does that sound?"

"Good." She laughed. "Matter of fact, it sounds great!"

They gathered wood and built a fire. John cut two forked sticks to serve as a rest for the spit to broil the fish over the open flames. He hummed while he cooked.

Kenda sat nearby, her eyes following his every move. He seemed relaxed and happy. "John?" she asked softly.

"Huh?"

"Why didn't they come with you?"

He jerked his head. "Who?"

"Your family? Why didn't they come with you when you first sailed to the islands?"

When he answered, his voice was sharp. "That hardly concerns you, Kenda."

39

She lapsed into a self-conscious silence, then after a while cleared her throat and asked, "Who are you?"

Now the jungle trees were all dim and insects cried out, and, sitting there waiting for him to answer, Kenda's thoughts slipped off in another direction. The *Beauty*. The boat would attach her to him. They would be alone, just the two of them, and the sea. He could not run from her or ignore her. There wouldn't be room. She seemed to have forgotten she had asked a question.

He turned the fish slowly. He hesitated, then said, "I'm an architect, but I've been in the construction end of the business for the past ten years."

The smell of smoke filled her nostrils. Occasionally a gentle puff of wind would change the direction and bring the blue smoke downward to where she sat. "What do you build?"

"Anything. Everything. Hospitals . . . malls . . . homes. We're versatile." He spoke while he dug under the ashes and retrieved the roots and yams he had covered up to cook. "How does this look?" He held the vegetables for her to see.

She shook her head. "I can't tell you. There are no words to describe how they look or smell."

He chuckled. "That's a strange reply from someone who memorized most of the dictionary. I would think you would never be at a loss for words."

"I memorized them, John," she said shyly, "but that doesn't mean that I know how to use them."

The meal was the most wonderful she had tasted in seven years. Maybe in her entire life. She ate until she was too full to move.

"Don't overdo it," he cautioned long after he had finished eating, and sat back watching her.

But his warning came too late. She had already overdone it.

Sometime later in the night, when her stomach had finally quieted, she drifted off into a restless slumber. Overdoing it had its rewards. After pouring the thick pink medicine down her, John had been afraid to leave her on the island alone. He brought a sleeping bag from the boat and made his bed on the floor of the hut with the declaration that departure from the island would be delayed another day since he couldn't start the trip knowing she was sick.

She tried to wear an expression of despair to match his, but for some reason she couldn't.

CHAPTER FOUR

Kenda awakened with a tiny ray of sun slanting across her face. She squinted and followed the beam to where it came through a small opening in the roof of thatched palmettos. In contrast to the night before, she felt extremely healthy. Gradually as she became more awake she jerked her head up and looked down at the floor. An empty sleeping bag was still lying on the ground. She laid her head back down and burrowed a little farther under the moss quilt, allowing her eyes to close again lazily.

"Kenda?" John stood in the opening, watchful eyes on her.

She opened her eyes.

"How do you feel this morning?" he inquired with a tone of concern.

She yawned. "I think I'm better."

"Better take it easy today," he said hastily. "No need to ask for trouble." He stepped back outside and stated,

"I'm about finished with the repairs. If you feel like it, we'll plan on leaving tomorrow with the tide."

Kenda crawled from her bed. She walked around inside for a minute, then went out the doorway. "John?" she called out to him.

He stopped and looked around.

"Am I always going to wear this shirt and pants?" she asked, with some melancholy. "If so, we need to work out something so that I can wash them."

He laughed. "I'll bring you a change when I come back to shore. Okay?"

Smiling, she nodded.

For several hours that morning she sat quietly in the shade of a palm and watched him work aboard the ketch. It was a beautiful boat, with an aluminum mast for a mainsail that loomed as tall as a coconut palm. The vessel sat gracefully in the aqua-blue water of the lagoon. Kenda didn't know much about boats, but she could tell that *Beauty* was sturdy and seaworthy and she would not at all be afraid to climb aboard when the time came. But the time wasn't yet, and she was glad.

John rowed the dinghy inland early in the afternoon. He walked over to where she was sitting and gave a change of clothes to her. "Try these." He smiled.

Kenda reached out and took the pair of white shorts and white T-shirt. "Thank you."

"We'll get you some clothes in the first port city we come to. It'll probably be a couple of days after we set sail."

She nodded, then a question crossed her mind. "How will I pay for them? I don't have any money and I assume clothes still cost money."

He laughed. "I'll say. But I'll tell you what, I'll loan you the needed amount."

With little effort Kenda rose to her feet. "I'll go change," she said lightly.

"Good. I want us to gather some fruit for the trip. You'll need to take a supply of the foods you've been accustomed to eating. We don't want to upset your stomach again like last night." He shook his head in dismay. "I should have known better."

She touched his hand. "It wasn't your fault. I shouldn't have been such a pig." The mere touch of his hand under hers made her insides tighten. She fell silent and in the swaying shadow of the palm a feeling swept over her that almost made her panic. She looked up at him and wondered what he was thinking at that exact moment.

Staring down at her, he shook his head quickly and stepped back.

Her hand slid from his. But it was still there—the feeling like a two-way magnet between them, pulling them close. She had seen it briefly in his eyes and felt it on his skin when her fingers brushed the top of his hand as he edged away from her.

His eyes went over to the hut. "Go on, change your clothes."

Feeling weak and foolish, Kenda went to obey his command. She had let her mind run away with her with the suggestion that he had felt anything from the touch. She had read a meaning into something that wasn't there. She felt as though she had just walked into a stone wall.

After changing clothes, she walked back to where he waited, and without speaking ducked into the forest. She glanced back at him.

He hunched his shoulders and followed. His mouth was set in a thin line, his jaw jutting out a bit in some kind of unspoken determination. Without a word he walked close behind her, waiting for some signal from her to begin harvesting the food. "I suppose we should have brought something to put it in," he muttered.

Kenda smiled to herself as she watched him slip out of his shirt and tie a quick knot in one end. Then he shook it open like a paper sack.

He continued to mutter under his breath, "I suppose if you ran around here naked for years I won't get fatally injured by some insect or varmint if I don't have a shirt on."

Kenda ignored his mutterings, turning her attention instead to a large tree with a diameter of more than three feet with smooth grayish bark and numerous branches dressed in pale green leaves and bright yellow fruit.

John bent down and picked up one of the fallen pieces of fruit from the ground. He rubbed it against the leg of his jeans before taking a bite. "Ummm, sweet," he said, swallowing. "Plum?"

She fluffed her hair with one hand. "Yes."

He began filling the shirt.

"We'll need to get these last, otherwise the coconuts, bananas, and the rest will squash them flat," she said.

"Excuse me." He returned and in a flip of the hands turned the shirt upside down and emptied it onto the ground.

Less than an hour later they were back on the stretch of beach with the shirt filled to overflowing. John emptied the fruits into the dinghy and walked back to her. "Let's fill it once more to make sure."

46

Another hour passed. The dinghy, laden with fruit, vegetables, and nuts, sat firmly entrenched in the sand. John squatted and reached out into the water to wash his hands.

The urge was irresistible. Running up behind him, Kenda pressed both hands against his back and with one lightning-quick move, pushed him headlong into the water.

He came up spitting water and wiping his eyes. "That will cost you," he declared in a light threat.

She laughed out loud and began running down the beach, smooth and graceful as a deer.

He ran full force after her.

She shrieked, "You'll never catch me!" Well ahead of him, she dashed into the water and began to swim outward toward the reefs.

Not hesitating, he came after her.

An expert swimmer and diver, she maneuvered herself to stay well out of his reach. When he came within almost an arm's reach of her, she dove downward to the bottom of the lagoon, seated herself on one of the large tables of coral, and waited. She made a face at him through the crystal water as he approached, then began to dart her way back to the surface.

A couple of yards from the surface of the clear blue water he caught her foot. She kicked to free herself, but he would not let go. With one hand wrapped tightly around her foot he swam over her and caught her beneath the abdomen with his other. Together they popped like two corks out of the water.

She took in a loud gasp of air, then fought his body lock.

"Who would never catch you?" He laughed. "Who was it now? The one that would never catch you?"

The entire length of his body touched hers there in the water, and the two of them stayed afloat with treading movements in unison. He started to say again, "Who would nev—" But the words died in his throat. This time he had lost the battle.

Kenda didn't try to speak; she knew no words could slip by the tightness in her throat. At this closeness she could distinguish every minute feature of his face, down to the tiny mole near the corner of his right eye. Her face upturned to his, her heart went crazy with awareness. Her arms slipped around his neck and she could feel his breath on her face. His lips touched her cheek, then moved to her wet hair, then at last made a way to her waiting mouth. A flash of lightning and she was on fire. His touch, the feel of his hands, the fierceness of his lips, set loose a savage sensation deep within her that ripped a path through her body. She closed her arms tighter around his neck, entirely dependent on him to keep them from drowning.

Somehow he tore his lips away from hers and whispered, "Kenda, we must stop this. We must."

"Why?" she whispered in return, raising her head, not understanding. "Doesn't it feel good to you, John? It does to me. Let's not stop."

Abruptly he released her and began treading water furiously. He gave a shaky laugh. "Let's swim awhile longer. I haven't seen all on the ocean floor I'd like to see."

Her spirits sank deeper than the bottom of the lagoon. Probably deeper than the deepest part of the ocean. She sighed and, wearing a solemn look, swam out a few feet from him, then dove down again amid the coral and water plants. His words had hit her heart like a cold, wet knife and sent a stab of bewilderment through her brain. She had been held tight in his arms, felt his warm and wonderful lips on hers, felt the electric currents flashing taut between their bodies, but then something had moved him away from her. Some unknown obstacle had fallen between them. But what? She felt small and insecure as she swam among the orange-red coral formations and the sea creatures. She felt smaller than the little urchins, or the crabs, or the starfish. She felt smaller than a single grain of sand.

The two of them would plunge to the depths, then emerge to the surface in quick springlike motions for air, then plunge back to the bottom again.

On one trip up for air, John said, "I think I'll pick up a few of the shells for keepsakes. Want to help me?"

She nodded in grudging agreement. John seemed very adept and at home in the water, but she supposed all sailors had to be in order to stay alive.

They swam along the calm water of the reefs; an enchanting underwater paradise of bright colors. She stayed in the background and observed John weave in and out of the sea's flowerbeds. All about them swam brightly colored fish, some large, some small, some smooth and even-tinted, some striped with bright blues, reds, yellows, and greens. She swam up beside him when he started to reach down and pick up a shell mottled with golden specks. Clutching his hand, she shook her head and they darted to the surface for breath.

"Why did you do that?" he asked.

"Did you not recognize it?"

He shook his head. "No. What was it?"

"A cloth-of-gold cone, or maybe you've heard of it by its Latin name, Conus textile."

He wiped water away from his eyes. "Is that the one with the deadly little shellfish inside, the one referred to as the rattler of the Pacific?"

She nodded. "Yes. Daddy told me that many tourists have suffered fatal injuries from that little harpoon inside the pretty shell. It's more deadly than the stonefish."

He smiled. "I know about the stonefish firsthand. I picked up one on my last trip."

"You didn't!" she exclaimed, wide-eyed.

"Yes, I did, and my finger nearly rotted off to prove it." He held up his left hand and displayed a scar at the tip of his ring finger.

They enjoyed themselves in the water awhile longer before John looked up into the bright sky and uttered, "I suppose we should make our preparations to make sail in the morning."

Wordlessly she swam along the surface beside him toward the shore.

First he pushed the dinghy out to the *Beauty* and unloaded the day's harvest. While he was at the boat, Kenda began to gather the few articles she possessed and carried them to a spot on the sand directly in line with the boat. She sat down and waited for John to return with the small rowboat.

The very real prospect that tomorrow she would leave the island burst upon her. She got up and walked a short distance along the beach. She stopped and turned her back to the water and gazed at the island. A homesickness grabbed her. She would never see the valley again. She would never wind her way through the trees that mile or so to enter the splendid peaceful stretch of land with the warm, clear lake fed by natural springs and with the wild growth of vegetables that had sustained her life over the years.

She advanced to the edge of the trail leading into the trees. Then she reached out and touched a tall, elegant fern nearby and breathed in the perfume of the island. The feeling clutching her now was quite different from any she had known, and tears began to flow. It was true that she was grateful that John had come to this place, but she was also filled with an uneasy sadness. Civilization. The word half frightened her. People. The thought that she would soon be around people again scared her to death. What would she find in the new world she was about to enter? She knew the world she was leaving behind, but what of the one facing her? Walking a step or two down the path, she removed a ripe fruit with insides like wheat bread in appearance from the breadtree and held it in her hands. Then she turned around and looked again at the beach of pure white sand. Though she would see the island tomorrow, she still felt for some reason she was looking at it for the last time—really seeing it, really painting it in her mind so that it would be a picture she would never forget.

She watched the spray from the surf breaking over the low reefs beyond the perfectly still lagoon. However calm the sea and the wind, there was always the gentle roar of the surf, and that sound she would carry with her always. Tears were spilling down her cheeks. Here she had spent those last precious hours with her father. Today she held his memory as clearly as it had been the last day she spent with him, and tomorrow her island would become only a memory. She would hold it too, as clearly in her mind as a memory as it was at this moment a reality.

"Kenda, I'm taking your belongings on board," John called to her as he picked up a stack of books.

By now she had walked back onto the sand. She nodded.

"What are you doing?" he asked after a minute.

She shook her head. "Nothing."

"Come here."

Again she shook her head.

He dropped the books in the rowboat and started toward her. His face was red; his cotton shirt clung to his body with sweat as he walked in her direction. "What are you doing?" he asked again when he drew near her.

She would not meet his eyes. "Nothing," she whispered.

"Yes, you are. You're crying."

"No, I'm not. Something just got in my eye. Sand or something."

"Don't tell me you aren't crying. I know tears when I see them. I ought to, heaven knows I've seen enough of them."

"Maybe I was, but it's nothing important."

"Must be. Anything important enough to bring tears is usually important."

She lapsed into silence.

"Was it what happened out there?" He made a gesture with his head toward the water.

She shook her head.

"What is it then?"

Kenda didn't answer. She clutched the breadfruit, holding it tightly between her hands, almost as if she took refuge in its touch.

He searched her face for a few more seconds, then shrugged. "I'm not going to stand here and try to speculate. If you want me to know, I suppose you'll tell me." With that he turned and went back to the dinghy.

She returned to her thoughts of the island.

That night for supper they ate the breadfruit and bananas and drank coconut milk, sitting side by side outside the hut, overlooking the lagoon.

John Taylor was restless. He repositioned himself several times, finally took out a cigarette and lit it. "The sunset was beautiful, wasn't it?" he asked blandly, keeping her under close scrutiny from a corner of his eye.

"Yes," she breathed. Then her thoughts wandered off to the gorgeous daybreaks and sunsets she had seen over the past years. She wished she'd had a camera during the years. What photographs she could have taken! Suddenly she straightened. "John, do you have a camera?"

"Sure," he replied. "It's in the cabin on board."

"Do you mind if we take some pictures in the morning before we leave?"

"Not at all. Matter of fact I'll row out and get it now. It has an automatic flash. We might even wind up with a few decent pictures this evening." He stood and brushed the sand from the seat of his pants.

She smiled up at him.

"Well, that's a welcome relief," he said jokingly.

"What?"

"Seeing you smile again. For a while I thought maybe you'd lost them all."

"I doubt that anyone ever loses a smile, John. It's just that sometimes it gets buried under a lot of sad feelings and has a hard time surfacing—but it's not lost."

He searched her face in the moonlight and inhaled a long draw from his cigarette. He blew out the smoke as he walked down the beach, the smoke swirling white in the air behind him.

A frustrating realization came over Kenda that nothing was ever as simple as it seemed. John had come to the island and now he offered her freedom to leave. For years she had wanted to leave above all other wishes, and now she had to recognize in leaving she would leave a part of her life behind. A good part of her life—almost seven years. And now the bitter thoughts of leaving could only be sweetened by the knowledge that she was leaving with John. Remembering his touch when they came together in the lagoon set her head to spinning with the wonder of him. Then she thought sharply of the unknown barriers that separated them. In two days he had become her new world.

"I'm back," he stated, snapping her from her thoughts. "And I brought more than the camera."

Her eyes widened. "What?"

He tossed her a Coke. She caught it.

He laughed. "I thought we might drink to our forthcoming successful voyage." He pulled the top from the can and waited for her to do likewise. "Of course, I realize champagne would have probably been more appropriate, but due to the frail condition of your stomach, along with the fact that I don't have any champagne, we'll have to make our toast with Coke." He held out the can and she touched it with hers.

He knelt in the sand in front of her, burying both his knees. "Here's to you, Kenda. May you leave this paradise and find another one out there equally as beautiful." He turned up the can and took a drink.

Again tears welled up uncontrollably as she lifted the Coke with trembling hands. She took a sip and swallowed.

Reaching out, he put his hand on her elbow, bent over, and kissed her lightly on the lips. "When something beautiful ends, Kenda, it's always sad."

She moaned and buried her head against his shoulder.

CHAPTER FIVE

John and Kenda sailed from the island with the morning tide. John maneuvered the ketch a half mile out where the reef lay very low and searched for the narrow opening that had allowed him entrance into the lagoon. Cautiously he guided the *Beauty,* which drew six feet of water from the shallow lagoon between the reef, out into the Pacific Ocean. Every few seconds he checked the Fathometer which measured the depth of the water by sending radio signals to the ocean floor. Finally, after two hours of tedious navigating, he looked at Kenda and smiled.

She snapped his picture.

"How many does that make?" he asked, still smiling.

"I've lost count." She swallowed hard, suddenly feeling a slight queasiness in her stomach. The jerky, swaying movements of the boat, along with the water spraying across the bow, made her head spin.

John immediately caught the green glow her face took

on and, with a gentle sense of humor, said, "You better go down to the cabin and lie down awhile, Kenda. You look a mite peaked around the gills. It'll probably take you a day or so to develop your sea legs. It'll be smoother when we move a little farther on."

Rising awkwardly to her feet, she staggered down the steps to the twelve-by-eight-foot cabin that had been divided equally into two rooms, each four feet wide and twelve feet long. John had hung a canvas sheet along the highest part of the cabin which was six feet from the floor to the ceiling. Kenda slid past the curtain and fell onto her bunk, burying her head in the pillow. After a moment she reached down and touched the floor, pressing her opened palm flat against the boards as if to brace herself on the bed while the *Beauty* tossed among the swells.

Midafternoon John came down and checked on her. He stuck his head around the curtain and said, "Don't feel bad, Kenda, I found myself hanging over the stern about two hours ago. But we've hit smoother water, so I anticipate we'll both be in good shape before long."

"I hope so," she murmured, not lifting her head from the pillow.

He reached down and tossled her hair with his hand. "I'll make a sailor out of you, that's for sure. Wait and see."

Now she raised her head and looked at him. "Does that mean you're going to let me sail with you rather than turn me over to the American consul at Suva?"

He smiled. "I think so, that is, if you want to. I'll report to the consul that you're alive so that he can relay necessary information to authorities on the mainland, but I think I'll be the one responsible for taking you home.

After all, I did find you." He laughed. "And that gives me squatter's rights, or something like that."

She smiled bleakly and lowered her head again.

"I'll bring you something to drink in a while. It's real easy to get dehydrated out here," John said.

She didn't answer. Instead, she closed her eyes and put her hand on the floor again. She didn't know why he had changed his mind about dropping her off on the island, but she was glad he had.

The night was better than the day had been. By morning, when she awakened, she felt her insides were in their proper place once more. The queerness had left completely. She raised up and peered out the porthole beside the bunk, taking in a deep breath of air. The water swept by, a smooth clear blue.

John stuck his head in and asked, "You awake?"

"Yes." She smiled, quite aware of his dark eyes on her. She knew she looked a mess.

He entered her compartment and held out a glass of orange juice. "We'll keep you on liquids today and by tomorrow you'll be ready for bacon and eggs."

"Hmmm, sounds good." She took the glass of juice. "Thank you, John, you've been so good to me. I don't know how I'll ever repay you."

He laughed loud. "Oh, we'll probably think of a way." He backed out of her part of the cabin and she heard him opening drawers on his side. "When you feel like a bath, come on deck and I'll rinse you off." His hand shot around the curtain holding a plastic bottle of lotion. "This'll keep your skin from drying out."

She heard his muted footsteps on the stairs leading up to the deck. Crawling out of her bunk, she didn't find it too difficult to walk to the bathroom, where she brushed her teeth with the toothbrush John had given her when he divided his belongings with her. After using the ends of frayed vines for years to clean her teeth, the brush felt strange. She washed her face with soap and dried it thoroughly before picking up the hairbrush. She stared at her face in the mirror, holding her brush in a frozen position at the top of her head. She didn't realize how much distortion was in the lake's reflection until she stared at her light golden hair that fell much below her waist. She knew she was blonde, but she never realized it was tinted the color of the noon sun.

Touching her cheek with her fingertips, she wondered if the tan would ever fade. She was almost the color of the natives and her eyes were the exact color of the water sweeping past the porthole above her bunk. John had said in the first moments he saw her that she was beautiful. Looking at herself, she wondered if she really was, or if maybe unusual wasn't a better word. She could not remember ever seeing anyone even vaguely resembling herself. She bared her teeth for scrutiny. Then she smiled. They were as straight and white as John's. She crinkled her nose and pursed out her lips. Then she made several faces at herself before she brushed her hair. She liked her looks. She liked the person she saw in the mirror. It was almost like looking into the face of a curious stranger. But it was comforting to know that she lived behind that face. Feeling stronger by the minute, she brought the brush through her hair with firmer strokes.

Beside her bunk she peeled off the clothes John had given her and wrapped a bath towel around herself snugly; then she picked up the bottle of lotion.

Walking out on deck, she looked around for him. Then she became aware of the never-ending stretch of water before them. The view took her breath away.

"Looking for somebody?" The voice snapped her from her momentary preoccupation.

She whirled around. "I'm ready for my splashing," she said with dead seriousness.

He looked at her for a long moment. She was wearing only the towel, which concealed the middle part of her body, but not the tanned legs, nor shoulders and arms, nor the top part of her fully developed breasts. He stood motionless with his eyes pasted to her.

She squinted over at him against the glare of the sun.

"I don't know how this is going to work," he finally said. "Remind me to get the shower fixed when we get into port." A look of alarm had crept into his eyes. He leaned out over the bow, holding on to the rail with one hand and swooped up a pail of water, then moved to where she stood between the main and genoa sails. "Come close to the rail," he instructed.

She moved to the spot he pointed to on deck. Loosening the towel, she turned her back to him, then held the towel out behind her by the corners. She started to ask, "How am I going to wa—"

Splash! The cool water struck the top of her head and ran downward in torrents. She shook her head and began the question again, "How am I supposed to—"

Splash! It came again. She spit out the water that had run into her opened mouth. "John!" Again the bucket emptied on top of her head. "I think I'm clean!" she choked out. Pulling the towel back around her, breathless, and dripping all over the deck, she swung around and glared angrily at him. "Were you trying to drown me?" Her hostile words rang out. She spluttered, "If . . . if you were, you almost did!" She wiped the water from her face with one hand, holding the towel tightly above her breasts with the other.

"Was it that bad?" John asked with mock seriousness. "Did you really almost drown?" His lips softened into a humorous smile as he reached out his hand. "Here, let me help you with your lotion. We've got you past drowning; let's see if we can keep you from shriveling up like a prune." He watched her pouting expression in amusement.

She started to say something else, but didn't. Instead, glaring at him with blazing eyes, she passed him the lotion. "I need help only with my back," she instructed haughtily and flipped around, turning her bare back to him. Grasping her hair with one hand, she held it up and away from her shoulders.

He squirted a palm full of the thick creamy coconut-scented lotion and slapped it against her back.

She stiffened momentarily, but as he rubbed the lotion along her shoulder blades, she began to relax. There was a silence. She could almost hear her heart beating as John's sure, smooth hands traveled along the surface of her back downward to her waist. Her breathing noticeably quickened. Then she felt something warm and moist brush the base of her neck. For a moment she didn't know what, then when she realized it was his lips she had felt brush her neck, she froze.

A heavy silence hung between them for a long moment. Kenda bit her lip. She wanted to turn around more than anything, but some force within her prevented her from doing so. Then she felt his arms coming around her shoulders and watched them overlap each other over her breasts. Her hair fell. Her hand had become too limp to hold it another second. The long golden strands floated down in slow motion and came to rest across his arms.

Slowly he turned her around in his arms and kissed her lips with a light, fleeting movement, then he laid his cheek against hers. His length against hers in the lagoon had been the first real body contact, but this time, with nothing between them but the wet towel, she became aware of a very different feeling. She felt hot and cold at the same time.

His lips moved slowly along her face until they met hers. There came no tenderness with this kiss, only a bruising eagerness forcing her lips apart under his. She became lost in the sensations sweeping her body, not understanding what was happening to her.

His hands caressed her breasts, softly at first, then with a growing passion. A sudden physical ache in her groin grasped at her, and suddenly she began to pull away from him, half in panic, half in fear. "John," she gasped, "I can't get my breath."

He did not utter a word as his arms squeezed her tightly for a moment then slowly floated away from her like leaves from a tree floating down to the earth. He stepped aside, avoiding eye contact with her.

"John?" She still felt very strange and uneasy.

He cleared his throat.

As if drawn to him against her will, she moved a step in his direction. "John?" she said again.

He looked over at her and smiled, a seemingly painful

smile. "I—uh—I think you probably need to go down and dress, Kenda, now that you've had your shower."

"John, I love you." The words tumbled uncontrollably from her lips. "I know I do, but suddenly I'm afraid. I don't know why, but I am." She trembled all over.

"Kenda, what could you possibly know about love?" he said sharply, perhaps more so than he intended, for immediately his tone softened. "In many ways you're still just a little girl in a grown-up's body. It'll take time for your emotions to catch up, but they will someday." Walking toward the stern, he said nothing more. He looked out at the foaming water the *Beauty* left in her wake as she glided gracefully along the surface of the sea.

That night, after a day of little conversation, Kenda sat on deck, her eyes fastened on John who sat on the starboard side of the self-steering wind vane at the rear of the boat. His eyes were fixed on the horizon.

During the afternoon he had begun lessons in an attempt to teach her to navigate the *Beauty*, but after a few minutes excused himself from the cockpit and went down to his cabin for a nap. She looked at the various gadgets—the large compass, the chronometer, the sextant. She had observed his use of the last two to pinpoint their exact position in the Pacific. He also had a radio receiver that thus far in the voyage he had made no effort to use. She looked at the various charts he had strewn atop the counter and her eyes came to rest on a ledger. She opened the cover and read: *Beauty Logbook. Captain John Taylor.* She turned the page. The first entry read: *Time, 1000 hours. Sailed from port at this hour.*

Suddenly a hand reached over her shoulder and slammed the book shut. "Kenda, you don't read a ship's logbook without the permission of the captain. It's like reading someone's diary."

Embarrassed, she offered lamely, "I'm sorry. I had no idea."

He picked up the book and placed it under his arm and lifted a warning finger at her. "I don't mind you being in here, but don't experiment with anything, okay?"

She felt her cheeks burning as she nodded.

With the book tucked under his arm, he turned around and returned to his cabin.

And now, watching him ignore her completely, she knew that she had displeased him in more than one way today.

"We'll arrive in Suva tomorrow," he stated matter-of-factly after a while. Still he did not turn to her.

She tried to smile. "I suppose that's good news." A shadow fell across her face. "You aren't going to leave me there, are you, John?"

Almost beaten, he sighed. "No, but we will be in port a couple of days and then we'll leave there for Hawaii. Destination—Honolulu."

"Does that mean you're shortening your voyage just to get me home?"

"Not really," came his easy reply. "That's still plenty of sailing, anywhere from thirty to forty-five days. We'll stop by the Fiji Islands, then I don't plan to stop again until we reach Fanning Island."

"Where is that?" She was happy at least to be able to keep the conversation alive.

"North of the equator."

Catching the tone of his voice defrosting, her own mood

elevated. "Who minds your business while you're away?" she asked more cheerfully.

"I have three vice-presidents in the company. The chores are kind of split up among them."

"Are you the president?"

Finally he looked at her. "Yes. I founded the company. Taylor Construction Company of California."

A pause came and she got panicky. "How old are you?" she asked, fearing he would again lapse into the dead silence.

He answered with a monotone of resignation. "I'll be thirty-four in August."

Her mouth fell open with surprise. "You certainly don't look thirty-four. I would have guessed you to be more like twenty-seven or twenty-eight."

He chuckled low, a chuckle tinged with cruelty. "What would you know about thirty-four-year-old men, Kenda? You went from sixteen-year-old boys to me. What can you compare me to, those damn monkeys on the island?"

Taken aback, she fell speechless.

He smiled a crooked, wistful smile.

"You're making fun of me, laughing at me, aren't you, John?"

"No, it was sort of a joke."

"I didn't find it to be funny."

He shrugged. "Sorry, didn't mean to offend you, but the truth is the truth, Kenda. You did go from young boys in your life to a mature adult male." He stopped and sorted something out in his mind before continuing. "Did you ever have a real relationship with one of your young beaux? Other than maybe kissing him on the lips?"

She propped her chin on her fists, her face filled with disbelief.

"Did you?" he persisted, pressing her for an answer.

"No, I never had sex with one of them, if that's what you're asking. And I think that's what you're asking," she gravely retorted.

The answer seemed to quell his curiosity.

"How many women have you had sex with?" she blurted out loudly.

He jerked around and glared at her, but made no attempt to answer.

"I want to know. I want to know if you're married. I have the right to know."

His crooked smile lay dead on his lips. Without replying, he lifted his sextant to his eye and pointed it toward the horizon. "I'm divorced," he said harshly. He continued to measure the altitude above the horizon of the moon with the instrument and then added, "And engaged."

It struck her as she heard his answer that she could understand why he had been somewhat reluctant to discuss his personal life with her. Divorced from one woman, engaged to another, and sailing alone in the Pacific Ocean with a third woman. She wished now that they had not ventured into the conversation composed of straightforward questions and answers.

He lowered the sextant and rubbed the end of his nose. "My personal life is in a mess right at the moment, Kenda. That's why I took six months off and decided to sail alone, away from everybody and everything that reminds me daily of what a mess my life's become."

"But you're not alone now, John. At least *I* don't feel

like you're alone. I am somebody, you know. I am a person. The fact that I've been stranded on an island for several years doesn't change what I am."

He stood and stretched his tall figure. "We're right on course. What do you say to a good hot meal of Campbell's soup and crackers with a little fruit for dessert? I'll even bring out the bottle and fix a mild toddy for our bodies." He sounded light for the first time since morning. "Then," he continued, "we can come back on deck later if you wish."

"Okay," she agreed reluctantly. Her clear feelings were becoming so muddled she didn't know what to think or feel. All she knew was that the thoughts and feelings she had at the moment were making her uncomfortable.

After they had eaten the soup and had dessert of chestnuts and pudding, she chose a quiet moment to bring up the subject again. They sat in silence at the small Formica-topped table, which was securely bolted to the floor to prevent it from turning over when the boat tipped. The kitchen cabin was well lighted, and she was glad, for she did not wish to miss the expression of his face when she ventured into his life again. "Why did you divorce your wife, John?" she asked calmly, though her insides were quivering.

His eyes narrowed for an instant and his lips tightened. "Let's don't ruin a good meal, Kenda, if you don't mind."

Her eyes widened at him. "But I do mind, John. You're always saying 'if you don't mind.' Well, I do mind. Up until this moment I've been worried that you might leave me with the American consul in Suva. I feared that you would. But how do I know now that it wouldn't be best for both of us if you did?"

"What does it matter to you? Why *should* it matter to you? Regardless of what you and I become to each other, that part of my life will never be yours." He sighed and shook his head. "Besides, it's painful for me to discuss it. So if you don't mind"—he met her eyes straight on—"I won't discuss it."

"Well, then, will you tell me about the woman you're engaged to? Or is that too painful too?"

He smiled faintly. "Do you know that all women have some traits that are alike no matter who they are or where they are, if they're in the middle of society or if they're isolated on a remote tropical island. You all have some traits that are alike."

"Will you at least tell me her name?"

He pursed his lips, then sighed. "Lillian. Lillian Stedman." His jaws clamped firmly.

"How old is she?" Kenda asked after a second's hesitation. She felt she had the advantage of the moment so she would use it. Heaven knew it might never come again.

"Thirty." He spat out the one word.

"Is she pretty?"

"Very."

"What was your wife's name?"

"Barbara."

"Was she pretty?"

"Yes."

She inhaled a quick breath. "John?"

He raised his brows, his face quite expressionless.

"What's your little girl's name?"

In an instant he had bolted up out of his chair and left her alone in the kitchen without a single word, not even a "Shut up, Kenda." But he hadn't needed to say that, his eyes had fully relayed the message.

As she looked at his empty chair, she thought, *Why did I do that? Why did I pry into areas of his life that apparently he doesn't wish to share with me? Now he may well leave me on Suva. And I won't be able to blame him if he does.*

She forced her mind back to the present moment. John Taylor was hers for the moment. No matter how many women he had waiting for him elsewhere, he was hers for the moment.

CHAPTER SIX

Kenda went up on deck after him. She was sorry the exchange of words in the kitchen had taken place. She simply wanted, above all, to earn her own place in his heart, a place he would keep with him forever.

Walking up beside him on deck, she looked at him steadily. "I thought you said something earlier about toddies and bodies."

He glanced at her. His tone was pleasant enough when he spoke. "On second thought, it isn't such a good idea. Sailing is much like driving a car; it's unwise to drink and drive."

"Oh," she said for lack of anything else to say.

His tone became very serious. "I've noticed the barometer has dropped twenty points in the past couple of hours. We may be in for a rough ride ahead."

She looked out to see the swells whipping into whitecaps. "What do you think it is, John, a gale brewing?"

He shook his head. "I don't know. I turned on the radio receiver for a weather bulletin, but I couldn't get anything clear, just static." He reached out with one hand and braced himself on the rail when the boat suddenly rolled acutely to the left and clutched her arm with his other. "You need to go to the cabin, Kenda. It could get dangerous up here before long. Look how the wind's picking up."

"Can't I stay up here with you?"

He shook his head vigorously. "No. Go below—now," he commanded and began working with the sails.

Within minutes she glared out the porthole in wide-eyed horror. She could hear the sea pouring onto the *Beauty*'s deck. It seemed to her the wind was picking the boat completely up from the water and slamming it from side to side. It went on that way for what seemed like forever, but in reality was little more than two hours when John called down to her.

"Kenda?"

"I'm here," she replied weakly.

"I think we're past the worst part. We must have gotten in on the tail of a storm."

"Are you coming down?"

"No, I can't. When you're able, why don't you make a pot of coffee, but wait until we're under a bit smoother sail."

"I will," she yelled back at him.

She made the coffee at daybreak and carried a mug up to him on deck. The sea remained rough and she spilled half of it on the steps, but somehow she managed to make her way to him with what was left.

"Thanks," he said, lifting the mug to his mouth. He

yawned and stretched his shoulders. "It's been a hell of a night."

"I know."

"Were you scared?" he asked.

"Half out of my mind. I should be used to storms by now the way they seem to blow up from nowhere, but it's different when you're not on land. Goodness, when you think of how big this ocean is and how small the *Beauty* is, yes, I was terrified."

He was silent a moment, then he asked a strange question. "What do you think about the ocean, Kenda? Just exactly what are your feelings about all this water around us?"

She shook her head. "I don't know. I've never really thought about it."

"Well, think about it and give me your answer someday."

They sailed into the harbor at Suva that afternoon a little past one. The island sat shimmering like a green jewel in the brilliant noon sun. Kenda sat on deck and watched John bring the *Beauty* smoothly through the narrow harbor entrance, which extended several miles. There were no sails flying over her head; John had used the engine to bring the boat inland, keeping the *Beauty* dead center of the channel. On both sides of them Kenda could see the waves thundering hard against the coral reefs and sharp-pointed rocks.

Once inside the harbor John switched directions to starboard and in minutes killed the engine, allowing the boat to edge close to shore behind a large building covering the top of a hill. Looking up at the modern construction,

Kenda let her eyes travel over the entire length, taking in every board, every stone. It was both familiar and forgotten to her—the yacht club at Suva.

Almost seven years and it hadn't changed. It may have been larger, but the basic structure was still the same as it was that night she and her father dined in the club dining room. She could never have dreamed that night what lay in store for the two of them. She felt an ache now, a sharpness in her chest that grew more aggravated with the memories stirring in her mind. She looked a moment longer, then turned to the steps leading to the cabin, feeling a strong sense of confusion.

A few minutes later John came down. Looking at her, his eyebrows drawn together, he asked, "Kenda, are you ready to go ashore?"

She reached out and unconsciously gripped his arm. "Not just yet, John. I want to stay here awhile." Her bewildered eyes fastened on his.

He sat down on the bunk beside her and grunted. "The longer you wait, the more difficult it'll be. I know you're frightened, but you needn't be. I'm not going to allow anything to happen to you. Don't you know that?"

She nodded. "I know. But I don't want to go. Not just yet."

He threw up his hands. "All right, let's compromise. I'll go ashore and see the consul, then by the time I get back, you be ready to go. We'll go shopping, buy you some clothes, then we'll have dinner at the club. I'll get us a room on shore." He laughed. "And you can start getting your land legs back."

Her hand gripped his arm tighter. "John?"

"What is it?"

74

"You think I'm being stupid, don't you?"

He rubbed the lobe of his ear thoughtfully, then met her eyes with a sobering frankness. "No, not stupid, but you're evading the real issue here. You're afraid to meet people, you're afraid to come in contact with the people out there on the island, and that's a problem I can't solve for you." He inhaled. "But you have to realize that you never wanted to spend the rest of your life on that island. And I think when you come to grips with that fact, you'll be better able to meet the problems you'll face now in returning to civilization." With that he lifted her chin with one finger and kissed her—an almost fatherly kiss.

She looked at him, a puzzled expression on her face.

He smiled, reached over, and patted her knee, two quick little pats. "I'm going now. I should be back for you in less than an hour. Be ready."

Watching him disappear behind the curtain, she knew she was madly in love with him. She loved being in his presence, watching him move, listening to the tone of his voice, seeing the way his dark eyes changed expression. He was gallant and handsome and wonderful. In her heart was all the joy of love, but in her mind she felt sadness.

She moved restlessly, half disturbed by what lay ahead when she went on shore, half disturbed by her feelings for John Taylor. She hoped they wouldn't be on land for any length of time. She would rather be alone with him on the *Beauty* than shop for clothes or dine at the yacht club or sleep in a hotel room.

She drew her legs up on the bunk and wound her arms around her knees, hugging them close to her body as if to ease the turmoil in her mind. After a while she composed herself and changed into the dark navy pullover and jeans

John had given her. Then she brushed her teeth and combed her hair.

Two hours later, smoking a cigarette, John rowed the dinghy back to the *Beauty*. Kenda had spent the best part of the last hour on deck watching for him. He climbed on board, then came to a standstill and looked at her. He wasn't smiling.

She went toward him with ease. "How did it go, John?"

"Not worth a damn." Anger flared in his eyes. "You could say I put the man in a total state of confusion." His mouth tightened and the gold glints in the brown irises burned brighter.

"What did he say?"

He drew an impatient breath. "Nothing that made any sense."

Her mouth dropped in bewilderment. "You mean he wasn't happy that you found me?"

He considered his answer a moment before saying, "Happy isn't quite the word, my little darling. He was ecstatic, out of his head with sheer delight. Do you know the bastard lit two cigars. He had one burning in the ashtray on his desk and lit another. That's what the news did for him."

"You aren't happy that he was happy?" It still didn't make sense to her.

"Kenda," he said after a long pause, apparently still debating some dilemma in his mind. "You don't wish to be left in the consul's charge, do you?"

"No," her answer came quick and firm.

"Well, I have made that fact quite clear to Mr. Curt Chatham, the American consul. However, he does not share the belief that you are yet ready to assume responsi-

76

bility for any decision, and he insisted that I relinquish you to his charge. He further stated that he would make all the arrangements needed to fly you back to the States. And even so much as told me he would accompany you on the flight."

Kenda tried to picture the communication between the two men and she felt herself fill with chaotic emotions. John was so angry, yet from what she could gather from the conversation, the consul had only offered a helping hand. She had never seen John look like this or act like this, or call anyone bastard.

He seemed to have lapsed into a heavy gloom when he stopped speaking. He mumbled a word or two under his breath that Kenda did not understand. She felt dazed by his reaction. "Why are you angry, John? I don't understand."

He looked at her hard and long with the fierce anger now directed at her. "Don't tell me you don't understand what I'm saying, Kenda. Damn it. Don't you see what's on his mind?"

Shaking her head, she managed a weak, "No, I don't."

"He wants to exploit you. He wants to take you *himself* to the States. He wants to be in all the pictures that will be flashed from coast to coast. He knows a front-page story when he hears one. The man's not stupid. Whatever else he may be, he's not stupid."

"Oh, no," she cried out softly. It couldn't be like this. She tried to clear her muddled thoughts. She knew there would be some problems associated with her long absence from civilization, but she wasn't ready or emotionally equipped to start handling them now. Not at the very first place they stopped. She wanted to believe that John had overreacted to Curt Chatham's offer, but looking at his exhausted expression, she couldn't believe it. She shook her head and found herself saying, "Let's leave, John. Let's just sail away now, at this very minute."

The anger vanished from his eyes and he smiled. Then he shook his head. "No, we won't run away, Kenda. We'll face it now and we'll face it later—together."

The news had upset her more than she had imagined possible. Her hand trembled when John held it, supporting her as she climbed down into the dinghy. He squeezed her fingers tightly, then he lowered himself into the rowboat and reached for the oars. As he took them to shore, her eyes followed the movements of his arms intensely. Seeing the smooth, tanned muscles expand as he moved the oars forward, then relax as he brought them down alongside the dinghy suddenly made her feel awkward and out of balance. She thought of how those same muscular arms felt wrapped around her body.

Little drops of perspiration glistened above the neck of his T-shirt and she could see them springing up on his arms. Her heart began thumping against her ribs and warm sensations surged through her. She glanced up at his hair, which was now ruffled by the soft breeze coming inland with them. She wanted to reach out and touch him, touch his arms, smooth his hair, but she fought the urge and finally slid her hands under her legs and sat on them.

A soft surf foamed around the rowboat as they drew near to land. Two men were standing not far off on the sand from where the dinghy came ashore. They were both clad in khaki shorts and jackets, both wearing sandals. One of them had a dark, black beard.

John was frowning again when he helped her from the

dinghy. She stepped from the small boat onto the warm white sand and looked over again at the two men who now walked in her direction.

"Miss Vaughn?" one of them called out. It was the one with the beard.

Her eyes widened and she felt John's arm slide around her waist. "Yes," she finally answered.

"I'm Perry Caldwell with wire service. Would you mind if we took a picture of you for our papers back home?"

She opened her mouth, but was not given the chance to speak before she heard John's harsh "Yes, she minds. You may not photograph her."

His abrupt answer brought a quick spurt of anger to Perry Caldwell's eyes. "Wait a minute, buddy."

John immediately stepped between Kenda and the two men. "No, you wait a minute. Miss Vaughn does not wish to have pictures taken, not by you or anyone else."

Perry Caldwell's eyes widened. "I believe that should be Miss Vaughn's decision." He craned his head around John's broad shoulders. "Miss Vaughn," he began.

Kenda shook her head wildly. "No. Please, no pictures."

Caldwell's mouth flew open. "May I ask why not? Don't you think the people back home have a right to know about you? Aren't you being a bit selfish, Miss Vaughn?"

Kenda felt the quick sting of tears smart her eyes. "I—I don't mean to be. Really. It's just—"

"Leave her alone!" John lashed out. "Get away from her!" He stepped toward Perry Caldwell, who had begun backing away. "And don't you ever use that old people-back-home-have-a-right-to-know with her again. Where the hell were the people back home for the past seven years of her life? Did one of them give a thought or a damn about her! Hell, if they had searched the island like they should have when they picked up her father's body, she wouldn't be here now! So don't you push her, not one inch! If you do, I'll put that damned camera of yours in a mighty uncomfortable place!" Fists doubled tight, he stood nose-to-nose with the reporter.

Caldwell leaned backward away from John's threatening face. "Okay. Okay. Don't get excited, buddy. I didn't mean anything." He shrugged, then turned away and motioned for his companion to follow. "I'll get back to you, Miss Vaughn," he called back.

Kenda cut worried eyes up to John.

His lower jaw jutted out and he brushed the hair away from his eyes with an impatient sweep of his hand. "Don't worry about it, Kenda. He'll leave you alone." Then he repeated, "Don't worry about it."

She was still dazed when John led her into the boutique down the hill from the yacht club. She stood just inside the door and looked around at the clothes aligning the walls, so emotionally affected by the encounter with the news reporter she was unable to see any one item clearly.

A plump native saleswoman walked up to them. "May I help you?" She spoke perfect English.

Looking at all the clothes, Kenda lifted both hands and rubbed her face.

Again John took charge. "She needs a complete wardrobe—from undergarments out."

The woman's face lit up like a Roman candle on the Fourth of July. "Wonderful," she replied. "What size?"

Again Kenda swung around and looked at John in bewilderment.

His eyes sized her up. "Oh, nine I would imagine." He chuckled. "We'll start there. When you try them on, we'll see what a good judge I am."

"Undergarments?" the woman asked.

Kenda flushed and averted John's eyes.

Even he flushed when he answered, "Let her have size five panties and"—he paused, stroking his chin—"uh, I guess maybe a thirty-four B." He shifted on his feet, not looking at her.

The woman nodded agreeably and began removing boxes from behind the counter. "While I get the undergarments, look around and select what items you like, then go back there." She pointed to a doorway covered with a loud-colored floral curtain. "That's the dressing room."

For more than an hour Kenda tried on clothes. John's guesses as to size had been perfect. She looked at her reflection in the full-length mirror in the shop, then met his eyes in the mirror. "Tell me, how it is that you know so much about women's clothes?" She turned sideways.

A smile of admiration on his face, he answered without hesitation. "I used to be a lifeguard in the summer when I was in college."

She thought a minute. "I don't get the connection."

He laughed. "My friend Carl Hester and I were both lifeguards. We used to make bets on what size—uh—clothing some of the girls wore, other than bikinis." He turned a deep red. "I made a few bucks off Carl. He always imagined things to be bigger than they were."

She had stopped admiring the casual raw silk pantsuit she had on and turned to face him. "How did you know?

Would the girls just come out and tell you what size they were?" She wore a faintly puzzled expression.

He shrugged. "Umm, not exactly . . . but we had our methods. We'd strike up a conversation with them, sometimes I would say I was majoring in marketing and was doing a research paper on female garments. That was always the best approach. I never met anyone not willing to help with a research project."

"John"—she was dead serious—"you were a bad boy, weren't you?"

He grinned and winked at her. "Not too bad, not the way bad boys go."

She flipped back to the mirror and after examining herself awhile longer decided against buying the outfit she had on.

When they left the shop, both carried boxes under their arms containing one dress, one pair of casual pants and a shirt, four shorts sets, one pair of jeans, two long-sleeved sweat shirts, a Windbreaker, five pair of panties, five bras, two shortie night-gowns, and a terry-cloth robe.

Kenda was thrilled. "Where will we put it all, John? It won't fit in my two drawers."

"We'll find room. There are storage areas under the bunks." He laughed. "From here we'll go to the shoe store, and from there we'll go to the drugstore. You can purchase some makeup, lotion—anything else you might need. Be sure to remind me to get several tubes of Chap Stick." His eyes twinkled at her. "That ocean wind can play havoc with your lips."

At the drugstore John called a taxi to drive them to the hotel. Added to the boxes of clothes from the boutique were four pairs of shoes and two large bags from the drugstore filled to the top.

Sitting beside him in the backseat of the cab, Kenda looked in awe at all the boxes and bags. Delighted out of her mind, she twined her arm through his and pressed her head against his shoulder. "It's just like Christmas, John. I don't recall ever having so many new things at one time."

He glanced down at her and smiled, but said nothing.

Her eyes flickered up at him thoughtfully. "How much do I owe you? Did you keep up with all you put on that charge card? I know you spent seventy-four dollars and fifteen cents in the drugstore, but I've forgotten how much the rest came to."

"I have the receipts," he said casually. "I'll send you a bill when my accountant makes the final tally."

She gasped audibly. "You're going to involve your accountant?"

He doubled over with laughter. "Kenda, you are so naive. Of course not. I'm only joking with you. You don't have to pay me for these things. God, I'm just glad I'm the one doing this for you." Suddenly his mouth tightened and the golden glints in his skin became apparent once more. "Believe me, there are plenty of people that would love to take you on an expense-paid shopping spree."

"I'm glad it was you," she said in a small voice. She was relieved to see the taxi pull into the drive of the hotel before John allowed his earlier anger to fully return.

CHAPTER SEVEN

The hotel on Suva consisted of a main unit and numerous detached bungalows facing the beach. The adjoining rooms John had reserved for them in the main unit had a stone terrace overlooking the bay.

With a long sigh of contentment Kenda surveyed the room with its wide, heavy beams and massive furniture which included a four-poster bed. She sat and bounced on the bed after John had gone to his own room. She then walked over to the neat stack of boxes and decided against unpacking them except for the dress she would wear to dinner.

Next she went into the bathroom and clapped with delight when she saw the huge bathtub. She ran it full of water and sank down into it. Submerged to her neck, she lay back and closed her eyes, profoundly enjoying the feel of the warm water that engulfed her. She could have stayed there all night except for the fact that John had said he would be back to get her at seven for dinner.

She then got quickly out of the tub and looked at the watch on her arm. She reached for the towel and dried her face and waited to see if the second hand moved. It did. She breathed out a long sigh of relief, unfastened the watch, and placed it on the floor next to the tub. That fright took away some of the enjoyment she had felt earlier.

Quickly she shampooed her hair and rinsed it with a fragrant conditioner. She examined under her arms and then her legs. No unsightly hairs. But, then, she hadn't had any in years, not since that day on the island when she sat and pulled them out one by one. Afterward she had run into the salty lagoon for a swim and had almost drowned when the stinging began. It was like being stung by a bee in every body pore. She had walked around for days with red, irritated splotches, unable to lower her arms. But she finally healed, and the fine white body hair did not return.

She stepped out of the tub and wrapped herself in a thick bath towel and stood in front of the dressing-room mirror drying herself while at the same time giving her skin a critical once-over. Already the tan seemed to be fading in the areas that had been clothed the past few days. But then she dropped the towel completely and decided it was only her imagination. Satisfied, she applied deodorant and bath power, then pulled on beige panties and struggled a minute with the bra. It fit. A bit snug, but it fit. She brushed her hair and flung it back away from her face. Then she walked fitfully out of the bathroom. The bra was suffocating her. Again she adjusted the fastener and inhaled a long breath. Blowing it out slowly, she put on the salmon-pink sundress with matching short-sleeved jacket. She rubbed the soft material with her fingers. Next came the panty hose and shoes. She glanced at her watch. Six thirty.

She took out her makeup kit and applied a thin layer of earthtone shadow on her lids and a touch of mascara to the tips of the already black lashes. A bit of blush on her cheeks and a quick sweep of pale lipstick on her full lips, and she returned to her hair. She plugged in the hand dryer, turned it on, and began fluffing out her hair. She dried it and hummed.

Finally dressed, she fell into the large cushioned chair, closed her eyes, and waited for the knock on the door.

Seven o'clock—no John Taylor. Seven thirty. An uneasy feeling began to tug at her. She squirmed in the chair, then got up and walked out onto the terrace. She looked over at his room. It was dark. Her feeling of uncertainty heightened. *Where are you, John?* she wondered silently with a frown. She glanced around outside, then ran back into the room, an eerie feeling surrounding her.

A few minutes before eight she heard a pronounced knock. Before she could slide the chain a loud voice sounded through the heavy wooden door.

"Kenda."

"John!" she cried out. "I've been worried half out of my mind." She pulled open the door.

"Why?" he returned aggressively. "You knew I'd be here." He wore a white open-necked dress shirt and dark pants.

"But you're late."

"I know. I had to make a call to the States. It took

longer than I anticipated." He lifted his brows. "You look gorgeous." A sparkle came into his eyes. "Better than that, you're almost too damn beautiful to be real."

"I'm real," she said softly.

"I know." He smiled and reached for her hand. "How about dinner, my lady?"

The two of them walked along the stone path hand-in-hand around to the front of the hotel. Inside the lobby he led her into the lounge instead of going directly to the dining room. "Now we'll have that toddy for the body."

She smiled agreeably. "I don't know anything about it. You'll have to order for me."

The room was dark and fairly crowded, but they found a vacant table near the bar. Almost instantly the chatting within the room stopped and Kenda could feel eyes pasted on her from every direction. Self-consciously she slid into her chair.

Instantly a waiter appeared beside them.

John ordered, "I'll have a Scotch and water." He hesitated. "And bring the lady a dry sherry." He glanced around, then cut his eyes sharply at the waiter. "Do your patrons have nothing better to do than stare at us?" he asked with a tinge of sarcasm.

The waiter offered a lame, "Yes, sir, it's just that, well," he continued awkwardly, nodding at Kenda, "you are Miss Kenda Vaughn, aren't you, miss?"

Surprised, Kenda's eyes widened.

"Nobody means any harm, miss," the man apologized. "They just want to look at you. And you are something to look at, if I might say that and not offend you."

Kenda smiled. "I'm not offended," she returned softly, but she could tell that John was furious.

The waiter left and she clutched John's arm on the table. "Please don't get so upset, John."

"I'm not upset," he shot back. "Not at all." He fiddled with the napkin beside his plate.

And then, entering the lounge, came the most unwelcome figure of Perry Caldwell. He walked directly to their table.

"May I pull up a chair?" he asked while dragging a chair from the table next to theirs.

Neither Kenda or John answered.

Perry Caldwell sat down, turned, and called out to the waiter to bring him a beer. He turned back and leveled a gaze on Kenda so unnerving that she squirmed in her chair.

The drinks arrived and still no one had said a word.

"This is a nice place." Perry broke the astute silence. "I come here often. They have great draft beer."

Kenda sipped her sherry and shifted in her chair again. John sat still and silent like a statue.

Perry scratched his head. "Mind if I talk a little business?"

Kenda blinked. Still nothing from John.

Perry took the silence as approval to continue. "I have this paper on my wire service that's willing to pay through the nose for an exclusive on this story, and I mean through the nose."

"Ah"—John raised one finger—"that's a subject I've been thinking about—"

"Exclusive rights?" Perry interrupted with a broad grin.

"No," John shook his head. "Noses."

The reporter jerked his head to one side and his mouth flew open. "What?"

"Noses," John repeated. "I've been thinking about busting yours, buddy, all over your face."

Kenda gasped, her hand flying to her mouth.

Perry Caldwell did not seem overly intimidated by the threat. "Nah, you wouldn't want to do that. Then I'd have to sue the hell out of you, Mister President of Taylor Construction Company of California. Might be bad for business. You know, public relations and all that jazz." Confidently he winked at Kenda.

John started to his feet.

Kenda clutched at his arm. "Please, John," she cried out in a whisper. "Please."

John settled back in his chair. "Don't push me, Caldwell, or you might just end up owning Taylor Construction. What's left of you. And that wouldn't be enough to carry to work in a paper sack every morning." He inhaled. "If you can't understand that this is a difficult time for Miss Vaughn, then that's your problem. You're wasting your time, and you can tell your 'exclusive rights' client that Miss Vaughn isn't for sale."

"Have you ever considered letting her speak for herself?"

John threw out both hands. "Speak, Kenda."

There was a long silence. Both men's eyes were locked on her. Her eyes were on the glass of sherry. She wanted to say something that would end the confrontation between the two men—but what? She thought awhile more, forming each word carefully in her mind before she opened her mouth to say, "Mr. Caldwell, I'm having a difficult time merely wearing the clothes I have on at the moment. Please leave us alone. I can't imagine what your newspaper wants from me, but it isn't important. I don't care. I just want you to leave us alone."

John slowly closed his eyes. Perry Caldwell's leaped halfway from their sockets and he stroked his beard. "What did you wear on the island, Miss Vaughn? Didn't you have clothes?"

She shook her head. "No, I had a wraparoun—"

He interrupted hastily, "Were you naked the day Mr. Taylor found you?"

Kenda flushed brightly.

Perry gave a snorty chuckle. "You were." He gave another. "That explains a lot." He finished his drink quickly and got up. "Excuse me," he said. "I just remembered an appointment." He rushed away from the table.

Kenda leaned forward. "John," she whispered, "he's gone."

Dramatically John's eyes opened and he stared at her. "Hello, Miss Headline."

"What makes you say that?" She was astonished.

"Oh, let's call it a hunch I have about him."

"I didn't tell him anything," Kenda argued.

"No, but your silence did."

She shook her head wildly. "I—I don't understand."

He reached over and took her hand in his, turning her palm upward. With his forefinger he traced along the lines, saying, "I see a wanton amazon alone and naked on an island. I see a depraved American sex maniac finding her."

"John!" Kenda drew her hand from his. "That's not funny."

He lifted his drink to his lips for the first time and

91

swallowed a large gulp. "You're right, my darling, it isn't." He pushed the drink back. "Let's get out of here."

She agreed and they walked briskly from the lounge, out of the hotel, then slowly down to the beach, leaving behind the unpleasant moments and the stares. They moved into the darkness where only the surf met them. Stopping long enough to take off her shoes, Kenda caught up with John, who had walked down to where the *Beauty* lay anchored in the bay. Hearing the unhurried sounds of the water whispering upon the reefs in the distance, Kenda leaned her head against his arm. "John," she said, "don't be angry with me."

Smiling a little, he searched her face, then touched it lightly with his fingertips. "I'm not." He twisted a lock of golden hair. "To tell you the truth, I don't care what's said about me, but I hate to see you become a headline sacrificial lamb. And I'm afraid of it happening, Kenda. I really am. I'm afraid of what it'll do to you."

A sweet native melody drifted down from the yacht club on the hill. She knew he was right. Maybe he was wrong to become so angry with someone like Perry Caldwell, but all in all, he was right. "Let's leave tonight, John," she pleaded.

Someone at the club had started to sing; a deep baritone voice floated in the air around them. John sighed and lowered himself down onto the sand, then reached up and drew Kenda down beside him. She felt his hand on her cheek, cool and light, gently stroking back and forth. The thought of losing him sent such a stab of fear through her that she shivered.

"Cold?" he whispered.

"No," she returned. "I'm just having bad thoughts."

He took her in his arms and held her close, burying his face in her hair.

She felt her blood begin to race in quick response to his closeness and she became consumed with a passion far stronger than any she had known. She could feel John's rapid heartbeat firing against her chest. She cautioned herself to be careful, to weigh her feelings, to think. His lips covered hers and all caution, all feelings, all thoughts, drifted away and she was lost.

Then all at once there were people around. "John, we're not alone," she murmured.

He nodded, then put his head down on his knees and locked his arms around his legs. She could see the tremors running along his back. After a while he reached out and touched the sand, then brought his hand to his face. Looking at her, he turned on a quick smile and cleared his throat. "We never did get dinner, I don't believe." He reached for her hand. "I'm suddenly famished."

They stood and brushed the sand from each other, then walked up the hill to the yacht club. On the way up a new thought was forming in Kenda's mind, one that had not occurred to her before. An important thought. She would discuss it with John later after she had sufficient time to examine it thoroughly.

They were fortunate to be seated in a secluded corner of the large dining room in the club. The first course of clam chowder arrived. Both ate in silence, occasionally sneaking quick glances at one another. Then came the salad, fresh crisp lettuce topped with ripe tomatoes and dressing. The main course consisted of delicious trout amandine for Kenda and a medium-rare steak for John.

She watched him now, wondering why he had hardly

spoken to her since arriving in the restaurant. She took a bite, hesitated, then asked, "John, do you live in a house?"

Chewing, he nodded.

"What kind of house is it?"

He swallowed. "It's a fine house. Big and empty."

Amazed, she asked, "You don't have any furniture?"

His brow creased slowly and he almost frowned. "No, I have furniture. Every room is furnished with the very best money can buy, I might add. However, that wasn't what I meant."

Kenda caught her breath, then lapsed into silence. It seemed she had a special gift for never saying the appropriate thing.

Under the unabashed stares of the other diners, most of them tourists, John guided Kenda out of the dining room, his hand against the small of her back. They walked quickly to the hotel.

"My feet hurt," she muttered. "And this bra is killing me."

"Part of the painful process, my dear," John said rhetorically, "of recivilization."

Minutes later, completely nude, Kenda lay in bed, too full of food and feelings for sleep. Already the sounds in John's room had died away completely. She stirred, thinking of him stretched out in his bed. She wished she were there with him, beside him, both of them close and warm in bed together. It would be right; she sensed it would be right because she was in love with him, in love with everything about him. Suddenly, for the first time since he had knocked on her door that night, she remembered what he had said about a call to the States. Now she could feel that thread of doubt weaving in and out of her thoughts, leaving an intricate pattern on her mind.

I know him, she thought, *and yet I don't know him at all.* Why had he made the call? Someone must be important enough to him to talk with all the way from the Fiji Islands. But who? Lillian, his fiancée? Or Barbara, his ex-wife? Or perhaps it was his daughter. She felt strange thinking of John as a father. She wondered about the child. Did the little girl look like her daddy? Did she have big brown eyes and curly brown hair? Rolling onto her side, she continued her thoughts.

Outside her room she could hear the gentle roar of the sea. She suddenly felt very alone and for a fleeting moment had the insane desire to knock on the closed and bolted door between the two bedrooms, and when he would open it, run and jump into his bed. But even as she thought it, she knew she couldn't do it. He had not even bothered to kiss her good night, not even the quick fatherly kind that he sometimes bestowed on her lips. He had not touched her in any way, just said "Sleep tight" and left.

It seemed they had been together forever and when she mentally added up the time spent with him, it was hard to believe that she had only known him six days. Less than a week. The next day would be a week, their first anniversary of sorts. She smiled and nestled into the pillow. Someday she would give him a wonderful present. He had been so good to her even under the pressures he brought with him from his life back home.

She thought of the lovely dress she had worn during the evening and all the other bright-colored clothes in the dress shop. He had made her feel like a little girl, giving her free rein to pick out and buy whatever she wanted. She

95

was suddenly glad she had not picked the most expensive items. She had loved every minute of it; trying on clothes with him admiring and approving at her side.

She rolled over and sat up on the side of the bed and flipped on the lamp. Smiling, she began opening the boxes and removing items from the packages.

She heard a knock on the wall. Her eyes grew wide.

"Kenda, go to sleep," it said.

Solemn-faced, she closed the boxes, put down the bag from the drugstore, and walked back to her bed. Once again under the sheet, she smiled ruefully. Then she tossed and turned. She knew she should be exhausted, but she felt so keyed up, so full of emotion, she couldn't think about sleep. She thought of the coming days on the Pacific with John. She could hardly breathe. He was thirty-four, she would be twenty-four in eleven more months. That wasn't such a big age difference. But honestly appraising the age gap, she knew he didn't view her as twenty-four, or even twenty-three; he saw her as sixteen—except when she was in his arms. During those few times, she felt he knew her true age and ability. She was a woman with a woman's body and a woman's mind.

Inevitably she yielded to the heaviness that sneaked up in her eyelids. In those wonderful, floating minutes, when she was not yet asleep or fully awake, thoughts of the billowing sea, the deep, blue water, the sky, the horizon, all floated away with her. She fell into a sound sleep before she could think out the answer she would have to give him someday about the true love in his life—the overpowering, all-consuming, beautiful, beautiful sea.

There was no way for her to know how many light taps had sounded at her door before the one that awoke her.

Opening her eyes, she listened. At first, nothing. She closed her eyes as the tap started again. For a moment she did nothing but grip the sheet tightly in her hands. Then she heard a muted: "Kenda?"

Slowly she crawled out of bed, switched on the lamp, and reached for her robe. Slipping it on, she overlapped the front and pulled the belt up in a tight knot.

"Kenda?"

The voice sounded like John's and then it didn't. Curious, she made her way to the door. With her hand on the chain she asked, "Who is it?"

"Let me in," came the reply.

"Is that you, John?"

"Yeah, open the door."

Sliding the chain out of the catch, she turned the knob and opened the door.

A very drunk Perry Caldwell reached out and grabbed her.

CHAPTER EIGHT

Kenda tried to scream, but his hand immediately flew to her mouth and covered it before any sound could escape. Her eyes rolled at him in horror.

"Shh," he whispered in her ear. "Be a good girl and I'll take my hand away."

Terrified, she made no move. He reeked of alcohol.

He sneered, "Do you promise? You've got to promise not to scream, then I'll move my hand."

She was having a hard time breathing with his large hand over her mouth and nose. Finally she nodded and he released her. For a moment she did nothing, then she slowly made her way to the chair near the door and gripped the arms hard. She felt an overpowering fear.

Perry Caldwell pushed the door closed and stood just in front of it, his drunken face blank. He waved out to her with one arm. "I know what you're thinking, but don't think it. Don't call out to him for help. You don't need help. I'm not going to hurt you, and I might hurt him." He brought his arm around and patted the left side of his coat. "I have something here that would stop him dead in his tracks."

Kenda's mouth fell open with a gasp. Frantically she swallowed hard. She could not allow anything to happen to John. She wouldn't allow it. "What do you want, Mr. Caldwell?" Courage welled up from some unknown source.

"The same thing I wanted yesterday," he slurred. "I want some pictures."

"All right." She did not pause to think. "Take one."

He shook his head and grinned. "Oh, no, not here, baby doll. I want a picture of you in your natural setting; the sand, the water, and in your natural outfit . . . the one Mother Nature gave you."

"You know I can't do that!"

"It's your choice," he said smugly. "And your lover boy's fate. The pity is, you see, if I stay here in this room long enough, I know he's bound to hear us. You sure you want to see what transpires when that happens?" He shrugged. "As for me, I've got all the time in the world, but I imagine you're a bit short on time at this moment, Miss Vaughn. So tell me, what's it going to be?" His mouth curled up and he stroked his beard confidently.

She didn't know whether to believe him or not. But she could tell he was not in any shape to argue with at the moment. Nervously she bit her lip and clutched her hands together.

He pointed a finger at her. "And there's one more thing you need to consider."

"What?" Kenda asked in a defeated whisper.

"The little matter of your passport. I am of the opinion that you are on this island illegally, Miss Kenda Vaughn; therefore I feel it is my duty to bring this little matter to the attention of the authorities."

She stiffened. "That isn't true. I had a passport. The American consul knows I did."

He staggered back against the wall. "It's a few years out of date, wouldn't you say? Huh? Besides, if you've got one, let's see it."

She buried her face in her hands and fought back tears of anger and frustration. "Why are you doing this? What have we done to you for you to be so cruel?" She wiped her eyes with the back of her hand. "I know why you're way off down here, Mr. Caldwell, and even here isn't quite far enough."

His small dark eyes shot daggers at her. "You're my ticket back, baby doll. You're my big story. For three years I've been stuck down here, hopping around all these damn islands. Well, I'm sick of them. You're headline material, and we both know it. I asked you nice the first time and the second time but, baby, this is the third time, and I'm not asking, I'm telling."

She began to weep again softly. "You—you can't possibly gain anything this way. Surely you know that. Surely."

He started toward her.

She backed away from the chair, her eyes wide with fright. "What are you doing?"

"I guess we don't need to be in such a hurry after all. Maybe I've got more time than I thought." He moved closer.

"You better not come near me," she said, her voice

101

suddenly low and calm. "You had better stay away from me."

"Oh, really?" he snapped. "I'll come nearer, honey," he said, taking a step closer, "and you'll let me. You'll do a lot of things to protect your lover boy. Won't you?"

She was so frightened of the expression on his face she scarcely heard him. She had never seen such a despicable snarl on anyone's face. He stood right in front of her.

"You thinking about screaming?" he asked cunningly.

She put both hands up. "Get away from me!" she shrieked in a whisper. "Get away from me or I will."

He shook his head. "Nah, you won't."

Backed against the wall, her face was covered with contempt and disgust.

He reached out and touched the collar of her robe, running his fingertip just along the edge of the fabric, barely grazing her skin. "You must have been quite a sight when Taylor found you, honey."

She slid down the wall away from him and his slimy touch. She was surprised that she could conceal her rage and fear. *Please, please,* she prayed silently, *let me get out of this. Let me get out of this without John getting involved.*

He lunged for her and she writhed from his path, leaving him to stumble and fall on the floor.

In that instant the bolt on the door between the bedrooms came flying through the air. The door opened and John ran to where Perry Caldwell was struggling to his feet. John lifted him bodily by the collar of his suit.

Oddly enough Kenda ran over and grabbed John's arm. "Don't hurt him, John. Please, just throw him out."

He dragged the struggling intruder by the collar to the entrance door, opened it, and slung him well past the terrace. He stood there a minute, staring out into the dark, then stepped back and closed the door softly. Finally, wearing only dark-colored briefs, he turned to face Kenda.

She fell limply into the chair, too weak to cry.

John knelt beside the chair and reached up to push back her hair. "Are you all right?"

She nodded. "I think so. You were right, John. He is a terrible man." Her expression was one of total desperation. "We've got to leave here, John."

"We will," John assured her. "In a day or so. I don't believe you'll be bothered by Mr. Caldwell anymore. I expect he learned his lesson tonight." He took her face between his hands, his gaze warm and understanding. "We've got to get supplies. I've got to scrape the barnacles from *Beauty*'s hull tomorrow when the tide goes out; then we'll leave."

Kenda drew in a quick breath and insisted. "We must leave. He threatened to turn me over to the authorities because I don't have a passport. He will, John, I know he will."

"Ummm." He drew back and touched his lips thoughtfully. "I guess that fact must have slipped by the consul, otherwise he would have forcibly taken you into protective custody." He stood. "Get your things."

She leaped from the chair. "Are we leaving?" When he nodded, she began to gather boxes and bags under her arms.

A strange amusement danced in his eyes. "We can take time to dress, Kenda."

She was deaf to what he was saying, bent only on gathering her possessions as quickly as she could and leaving the hotel.

"Kenda," he implored her, "get control of yourself. No one's after us, not yet anyway."

"They will be, John," she said helplessly. "We must leave now—this minute."

"Okay, okay," he obliged her. "But I'm going to put on my pants." He winked. "If you don't mind."

Fifteen minutes later the *Beauty*, under engine power, was on her way out of the harbor, an extremely dangerous task to undertake in the middle of the night. However, a bright moon helped with the navigation of the long narrow channel. John waited until he had cleared the entrance completely before putting up sail.

Working with the rigging, he looked around at her sitting close by. "How does it feel to be a sea dog again?"

She laughed. "Better than being a landlubber. Much better." Suddenly the smile died. "I don't know if I ever want to see land again. We may just have to sail the oceans from now on."

"Oh, no, you don't," he cautioned her. "One bad experience and you don't throw in the towel. You're not a quitter, Kenda. That is one thing I know for sure. There are survivors, and there are quitters, and you, my darling, are a survivor."

The voyage seemed to be starting well and Kenda leaned back against the cabin wall and closed her eyes. Already she was realizing how poorly she had handled the situation with Perry Caldwell when John cleared his throat somewhat violently and asked, "Why did you open the door to him?"

Opening her eyes, her mouth dropped open. "Because he said he was you."

"I thought you knew me." He tied a knot in the rope.

"I'm surprised that you could confuse me with a man like that."

"It all happened so fast. I was groggy with sleep."

"Well, I regard it as a poor reaction to an emergency situation." He tied another knot and pulled the rope firmly. "You need to bone up on reactions."

She gaped at him, too astonished to say a word.

"The man was not that unique. There'll be others much like him." He rubbed his hands on the seat of his pants and eyed the sails. "And, Kenda, I personally would advise you against posing for any of them, regardless of threats, or large sums of money, or whatever. I think in the long run it would be to your disadvantage to do so," he said grimly. "People who reveal everything sometimes take the pleasure of wondering out of another person's life."

It took a moment for his words to sink completely into her mind. But when they did, they stayed. "John, you knew he was there, didn't you? You knew before you burst in."

"From the first tap on your door. For a fact, he woke me before he did you."

"Why? Why did you let me go through all that before you—"

"I wanted to see how you handled yourself in a crisis, Kenda."

She became furiously silent. Her shoulders were quivering.

"Why don't you grab a few winks of sleep. We still have several hours of darkness."

On her bunk she shook her head buried in the thin pillow. She cried softly for a long time, thinking black thoughts, feeling the *Beauty* toss gently under her.

* * *

Kenda stared out her porthole in the early morning at sunrise watching the ocean. Her insides felt like ice, and every now and then she could feel an inward shiver. Slowly she dressed in her new denims and long-sleeved white sweat shirt to protect her against the cool morning air. Still recalling the events of last night, she realized she was wrong in the manner she had handled the reporter's late-night visit and threats. But was she more wrong than John to allow it to take place? She moved toward the bathroom, aware of the biggest letdown she'd faced so far. She was freshening up when she heard John call, "Breakfast."

Giving her hair one last sweep with the brush, she turned and went out of the cabin and into the kitchen. She took her place at the table and murmured a low, "Good morning."

Across the table, John snorted, "Did you wake up a grump this morning?"

"No," she said lightly, "not at all." She lifted the mug of coffee to her lips, and just as she did the ship rolled and the coffee splashed against her mouth, running down her chin and onto the front of her new shirt. When she caught the smug little smile on his face, she threw the mug to the floor and bolted from the table, striking her head against the ceiling.

"Temper . . . temper," he cautioned, taking a bite of scrambled egg. He raised his brows at her and swallowed. "Eat your breakfast."

She swung around and glared wild-eyed at him. "I will not!"

"Yes, you will." He motioned to her chair. "Now, sit back down and eat your breakfast."

She tried to keep the tremors from her voice. "You cannot order me to eat as if I were a child. I'm not hungry, therefore, I will not eat!" She hastened from the doorway and up the steps to the deck.

She expected him to come after her. She crossed her arms across her chest and waited, leaning against the mast of the mainsail. But he didn't come. After a while she climbed down and took a seat on the bench at the boat's stern. She felt a strong surge of disappointment. A tear slid down her face, but she quickly and angrily brushed it away.

After a while John appeared on deck and stretched. "While everything's shipshape I think I'll go grab forty winks." He stretched again, baring his dark stomach between his shirt and khaki shorts. She looked at the sun-bleached growth of hair around his navel. She had seen it before when he didn't have a shirt on, but for some reason it looked different exposed between his shorts and shirt.

He glanced at her quizzically, and at the same time pulled at the bottom of his shirt. "May I ask what you're doing?"

She sighed. "I was merely looking at the hair on your stomach."

"Well, do I go around glaring at the hair on *your* stomach?" he fired back.

"I don't have any."

He gave an exasperated snort. "I see you're not wearing your bra. How would you like me to stand here and glare at your breasts? I can see the brown spots through that shirt—three, counting the coffee stain."

Before the sound of his words vanished, she again sat with her arms folded across her chest. Now she was more confused than angry. My Lord, she couldn't believe anyone could get so upset because someone looked at their stomach. Nothing was making sense anymore.

He snorted again. "I'm going down to sleep. Your breakfast is still on the gimbal tray beside the stove if you decide nutrition is more important than temper tantrums." He quickly disappeared down the steps, followed by a loud thud.

She smiled, knowing he had struck his head on the ceiling just like she had. Now who was having the tantrum? Her smile broadened.

After he had gone, she got up, walked around on deck awhile, then went down to the kitchen and took her breakfast from the gimbal tray which stayed level regardless of the rolling or tipping of the ship. After she had eaten, she cleaned up the mess he had created when cooking the meal, glad it hadn't been a big kitchen with lots of pots and pans.

She started back topside, then stopped and tiptoed to the cabin. Without making a sound she pulled the curtain back and sneaked a peek at him. With nothing but his shorts on he had stretched out stomach down on his bunk, his head turned to the curtain, one arm hanging limp against the floor. She looked at the relaxed muscles across his back, the smooth and even rising with each breath. She had a battle with herself to keep from reaching down and touching the auburn ringlets around his neck. What a temptation not to just lie down beside him and slide out full length, feeling her breasts against his back, her thighs against his thighs, her legs entwined with his. There was a strong feeling between them. She knew there was, and they could fight it for the thousands of miles above the bright blue water or give in to it and float away into a world of their own. She squeezed the curtain tight, then dropped it, and tiptoed back on deck.

It was midafternoon before he came up. She had just looked at her watch. Three o'clock. Tiny specks of water had gathered under the crystal after submerging it in the bathtub, and she was relieved to see they had vanished and the hands ticked on as though they had never had a bath. She loved the watch. Above all other things he had bought her, she loved the watch best. It was big and kind of gaudy, with a large black face that supported three hands in a silvertone case, strapped on by a wide black band.

The afternoon was perfect. A perfect day with a brilliant blue cloudless sky and sunshine beams bouncing off the *Beauty*'s sails and dancing brightly along the water's surface. There had never been a more perfect day.

"Have you kept us on course?" John asked, starting to stretch, then changing his mind. He just kind of wiggled his back and shoulders.

Kenda stared at him. "Of course, I've kept us on course. What did you think I would do, sink the boat just so you couldn't get your nap." She smiled.

John grinned at her. "I see you're still the same tart I left on deck." He walked into the cockpit, was gone a few minutes, then reappeared. "I've had to rechart our course home. We'll stop by Apia on the Samoan Island of Upolu for supplies and water, and I've got to clean *Beauty*'s hull."

"How long will it take us?"

John wrinkled his nose. "Not more than a couple of

days. We won't vary much from our original course. We've already come over a hundred miles since leaving Suva, which is great considering we still have much of the day left. If this weather and wind keeps up, we may set a record for a yacht sailing this distance."

Kenda looked quickly away, pretending to be interested in the view of the horizon. He seemed pleased that the voyage might be shorter than anticipated, but she wanted it to be as long as possible. She felt her disappointment rising.

"I think you'll need to stay aboard at Apia, Kenda. I'd hate for us to encounter anything there like on Suva." He gave a short laugh. "I'd hate for someone to end up taking you away from me."

"I'll bet." She laughed ruefully. "I'll bet it would break your heart."

"It might."

She hesitated a moment, then asked, "Do you love me, John?" How easily the question had come, almost on its own.

"What is love?" he asked in answer, walking over and placing his hand around the boom. "Tell me what it is, and I'll tell you if I do. Deal?"

"That's crazy. What am I supposed to say—the dictionary definition? I know it. You want to hear it?" Her words tripped out, running into one another. "Love, noun form, a deep devotion or affection for another person or persons: example, love for one's children—"

"Okay, okay." He threw up his hands. "Maybe you know the definition and maybe I don't." His hand tightened on the boom. "Barbara used to say I loved the wild wind." He hesitated, then to Kenda's surprise continued.

110

"Of course, she was making light of my sailing, my love of the sea. She hated it. Never sailed a foot from shore with me. If it hadn't been for Jill, she would never have even seen the *Beauty.*" He suddenly stopped talking, dropped his hand, and walked back into the cockpit.

Kenda had seen her first glimpse into his deepest feelings and she found herself at a complete loss to handle her own. She had asked him if he loved her and he had wound up talking about his wife and child. Jill. It had taken a week, but she at last knew the child's name. A little girl named Jill had christened the *Beauty.* John had a little girl named Jill.

For the remainder of the day he was depressed. Kenda had not expected the abrupt change in his mood, and try as she could to understand it, she couldn't. If the mention of his wife and child lowered him into these depths, perhaps he still cared, maybe even more than he chose to admit to himself. After a while her own mood became pessimistic. She loved him. Of that fact she was certain. But, that he loved her, she was doubtful. How could he, and allow the mention of his past life to drop him into a sinkhole?

Resolutely she declared in silent promise that she would never again mention love or family or fiancée. It seemed to her, whenever she did, all she accomplished was the opening of another Pandora's box.

All of a sudden she saw visitors off the bow. A school of porpoises were swimming and diving in the water ahead. Watching the creatures have such fun, squeaking and talking to one another, lessened her own miserable feelings of the moment. She watched until they were al-

111

most completely out of sight before turning around to look at John.

He, too, had been watching the sea creatures at their fun and games from where he stood outside the cockpit. He smiled bleakly. "You can't imagine what company dolphins are when you're alone out here. I've had them come so close to the boat that I could have actually reached out and touched them. It's amazing how happy and fearless they are, as if they know everything about everything, and are satisfied with their knowledge."

Her lips smiled in return, but her heart didn't smile, nor did her blue eyes.

He walked over and sat down beside her. "You want me to teach you how to sail?" he asked with an obvious attempt to be light.

"Yes," she returned readily. "I want to learn it all. Someday I may have my own boat and set out to catch my own wild wind."

He squeezed her hand. "After we leave Apia, I'll teach you."

"Promise?"

"I do, and, madame, when I make a promise, I keep it."

"I'm going to count on that. Regardless of how bad a student I am, or how slow I am to learn, you have promised to teach me."

"And that I will," he said with assurance.

CHAPTER NINE

Apia was bypassed when several miles out at sea Kenda and John overheard radio conversation between two British coast guard ships that the yacht *Beauty* had been sighted in the direction of Apia. One radioman had then asked if that was the yacht carrying the "mermaid" rescued from the island below the Fijis. When the other ship had replied affirmatively, John had immediately altered his course, hoisted sail, and headed straight out to sea again. He had been doubtful that he could have cleared himself with the custom officials, and now after hearing the coast guard banter, he felt it would be impossible.

The main concern was the water supply. While Kenda ran inventory on the food, he measured the fresh water in the tank. Twenty-eight gallons remained in the fifty-gallon tank. Taking out a pencil, he calculated out loud. "That should be an adequate supply for—uh—let's see, six weeks." He looked over at Kenda, who was counting cans under the counter of the sink.

"There are fifty-one cans in all," she called up from her crouching position. "Six pounds of dried beans and rice, half a sack of oranges, ten apples, most of the potatoes in your bin." She looked over to the wooden box still half-filled with fruit and nuts from the island. "And that," she said, pointing to the box. "Plus we have plenty of coffee, tea, and powdered milk, flour, and sugar."

He looked pleased. "That should do it. We can get out the fishing gear and start catching our protein. There are still close to two dozen eggs in the freezer, and butter and bread." He laughed. "We may even gain weight."

She sat on the floor. "What about the barnacles? I thought you said they needed to be cleaned from the hull."

"True. I'll have to do that one day soon. We can drop anchor near one of the more isolated islands and I can put on diving gear and take care of my botanical garden growing on the hull."

"Can I help you?"

"Ummm, probably not. You might be too much of a temptation for the sharks. They won't bother with an old scoundrel like me."

Her eyes grew wide. "You're not going in water where sharks are?"

"Not if I know it; however, they have a habit of sometimes concealing their whereabouts."

"Why can't you leave the hull alone? What does it hurt to have a few creatures growing on it?"

"If enough grow, it can affect our maneuverability and balance."

* * *

114

Several days later when she walked out on deck she felt a mixture of optimism and awe. Since John had begun the sailing lessons their relationship had suddenly changed. Teacher—pupil. Rarely, if ever, did he touch her in any way. It was almost as if physical contact were in violation of the rules of learning to sail. They were getting along fabulously. Few cross words passed and in teaching her he had the patience of Job.

He came up and sat down beside her near the railing and softly drummed the metal rail with his fingers. "Have you checked our course?" he asked matter-of-factly.

"Yes," Kenda replied. "Also the logspinner. It has recorded a hundred and twenty-six miles since this time yesterday."

John stretched his legs out full length on deck. "Did you get a sun fix to check the accuracy?" Then he cautioned with, "Remember, I've told you never to depend entirely on man-made instruments."

"I did get a sun fix and the recorder was right."

John smiled. "Good. That's an A." He raised his brows at her. "You do realize that the wind is at our backs, don't you?"

Kenda nodded. "Yes."

"Are you ready to try a little butterfly sailing?"

She nodded anxiously. The ship was taken off automatic pilot and, manning the tiller, Kenda swung the mainsail out to the right of the *Beauty* and the jibsail to the left. The *Beauty* suddenly looked like a big butterfly scudding along the water in a smooth, fast motion.

Suddenly the wind shifted from astern to southwest and the *Beauty* swung abruptly to the right and began to flounder. John jumped to his feet and began to struggle to pull in the sails. He was nearly swept overboard before he managed to haul them in. When the *Beauty* was redirected on course, he veered his eyes toward Kenda, who sat petrified.

There was a long painful silence, but she was determined not to give in to his accusing glare. "How was I to know the wind would change like that?" she offered lamely. "We were breezing along beautifully. How did I know the wind would suddenly change its mind?"

"And that, my dear, is one reason why Davy Jones's locker is so full of half-ass sailors." He pounded his fist against the thirty-foot mast of the mainsail. "You have to be able to second-guess the sea and the wind if you plan to conquer it. You have to be strong, your mind has to be quick, and you have to become a part of the nature around you. You can never take anything for granted. Never." He raised his brows at her. "And that's a D minus."

She screwed up her face at him and jumped up. "Damn your silly old grades! I don't care if its an F—a triple F. I was doing the best I knew how. You haven't taught me everything yet, Professor Perfect. You taught me how to sail wing to wing, but you didn't teach me what to do when the stupid wind changed. So there!"

Throwing back his head, he laughed long and hard.

Stomping toward the cabin, she swung around viciously. "Laugh all you want, Captain Smartie, but I'll tell you one thing. By the time we get to Hawaii, I'll be able to sail the pants off you. Wait and see," she snapped back at him.

He stayed on deck a few minutes, then followed her downstairs. He stuck his head into her compartment. "Is this a mutiny?" he asked, still laughing.

She didn't answer.

116

He sprang inside and grabbed her. "I asked if this is a mutiny."

She grinned, her eyes sliding over his face. "What if it is? What are you going to do about it?"

"I have my own method of handling mutineers."

She raised her brows. "Really, and just what would that be? Throw them overboard?"

"Oh, no." His face grew close to hers. "Nothing so nice as that." Drawing back from her, he pulled his T-shirt off.

"In that case you'll have to show me. I am definitely a mutineer," she said breathlessly.

He smiled and closed the distance between them as his fingers tightened on her shoulders. Now he was half frowning, half smiling; his eyes had a strange gleam in them. His mouth, hot and moist, traced a path across her cheek, then found her lips frantically. "I need you. God, I need you," he murmured, his lips brushing hers.

A shuddering excitement passed through her and she felt her strength ebbing away like the morning tide. Weakly she sank down onto her bunk, her arms tight around his neck, pulling him with her.

She suddenly felt her shirt sliding up over her head, then falling to the floor. The touch of his naked chest against her breasts completely shocked her. It felt as if she'd been licked by a tongue of flame. His lips traced a burning path from her mouth down her neck, then across her breasts. Her body blazed while her mind screamed in denial. No! No! A deep fear began to emerge. "Please don't, John," she whispered in a half sob.

He lay perfectly still for a moment, his body pressed hard against hers, then he raised his head and looked in her eyes. A second later he was gone, not bothering to pick up his shirt from the floor.

She wanted to die. She wanted him desperately, but not this way. Not without love. If making love would make him love her, then she would have never protested, not in a million years. There came the fear. That he needed her, desired her, could not be argued; that he loved her was debatable.

"Oh, John," she moaned half aloud. "I don't know which is worse, to have you ignore my body or to have you touch me. Both torment me." She reached down and clasped the shirt on the floor and slipped it quickly over her head, sobbing in dismay.

When she returned on deck an hour or so later, he sat busily mending a sail. The encounter was not mentioned by him in any way. It was as if it had never happened.

"John," she began.

"Let's forget it, Kenda." His voice wasn't harsh or ugly, just firm. "You need to sweep out the cabins while I finish these tears."

Several hundred miles south of the equator, on the twelfth day out at sea from Suva, a black squall blew up on the horizon.

John was back to his factual self. "We need to reef the sails, Kenda. We can expect an increase in wind velocity shortly." His eyes did not leave the black cloud.

Almost immediately the sea began to get rough. The sails were completely down except the jib, which was not larger than a small tablecloth. John threw a harness to her, which she fastened on like a vest, and he did likewise. By that time the swells were coming in fast, smacking the

Beauty fiercely against the stern, spraying water from the crests that covered the ship, and slamming halfway up her mast. Water sloshed on the decks and ran down into the cabins.

Blackness covered the sky. Loud, deafening thunder rolled continuously across the darkness while shimmering streaks of green lightning flashed without end.

John sat with his arms firmly around the tiller.

"Can't we switch to the motor?" Kenda screamed out above the thunder. A huge swell washed over and drenched her, slamming her to the deck floor. She slid toward the rail until the rope to the harness stopped her. She tried to get to her feet.

"Get below!" John yelled out, taking one hand from the tiller to motion to her. When he raised his hand, the boat began to pitch to the right and he fought frantically to prevent the sideways turn that would roll them over into the angry sea.

On her hands and knees, Kenda crawled to the cabin to find the floors under several inches of water. She began pumping it out, and as soon as she could see progress, another wave would hit and fill the floors again.

The storm lasted three days. Many times during those dark hours Kenda felt that the two of them and the groaning, shuddering *Beauty* would not make it to see another bright sunny day. Neither slept. There were times when she would pass out from exhaustion, but she would always wake up again in a few minutes to find the swells had grown even larger than before she lapsed into unconsciousness. Water sloshing about her ankles had become a way of life. She could hardly remember what smooth sailing had been like.

On the third day she did manage to get a thermos of coffee up to John. He looked terrible, beat and haggard, his eyes hollow from lack of sleep.

"How're you making it?" his voice slurred at her.

"I'm making it," she returned, trying to sound as strong as she could. She slid down beside him.

"It can't last much longer," he said before taking a big swallow of coffee from the thermos.

"We can't either," she said solemnly. "Neither can the *Beauty*."

Water sprayed over them and she wiped her face with her arm. "John, let me **stay** awhile. You try to get some rest."

"No. I'll stay here. Nothing can happen to her, you know. I won't let it."

"Who? The *Beauty*?"

Delirious from lack of sleep he began to ramble. "The *Beauty* is unsinkable . . . like *The Unsinkable Molly Brown* . . . you remember her . . . nah . . . you couldn't. It was a Broadway show about a lady who was unsinkable . . . Molly Brown. I was going to name her Molly Brown, but Jill, my Jill, wanted to name her *Beauty* . . . after her favorite story . . . 'Black Beauty.' She wanted to paint her black. I told her I couldn't, she was fiber glass." His eyes were rolling up, then down, his head nodding. "I would have painted her black, I would have done anything . . . I would have done anything . . ." His words began to slow. "Anything . . . anything."

"John!" Kenda screamed, grabbing his arm and shaking it. "What's the matter with you!"

He passed out cold, slid from his seat, and lay motionless on the deck.

Kenda screamed. She was a bundle of nerves—the storm, the days without sleep. "John, get up!" As she spoke, she slid into his seat and groped blindly for the control of the *Beauty*. With a supreme effort she fought to keep the boat from corkscrewing after sliding down one of the huge swells. The sea swept over her and the fury of the storm surrounded her. How they were still afloat was a miracle.

Suddenly she was no longer frightened. She was too tired to be frightened. Even with the deafening noises roaring about her she felt a strange silence inside her. The panic had gone and in its place came a calmness. When the storm began, she had been certain they would survive it, that it would pass leaving them unharmed. Now the crazy thought crossed her mind that they would not survive. In the test of strengths, the sea would win. Scenes of the past days, bright flashes of her moments with John Taylor began to surface. Wonderful minutes, wonderful hours, wonderful days.

She peered down at his soaked body at her feet and she didn't feel so very alone. Weary, but not alone. Then suddenly she left the tiller and crumpled to the floor next to him, placed her arms around him, and pulled him very close. In an effort to give herself courage for the coming moments, she whispered to him, "We did the best we could, my darling. You want to know what I think about all this water around us, well, I think she's been good to us, all in all. She's stronger than we are. I hate to admit it, but it's true." Then she began to cry, not so much out of sadness. She knew her moments of consciousness were ending. She closed her eyes and the noise around her became even more distant. She remembered nothing else.

* * *

When she awoke she found herself lying on her bunk. For a moment she couldn't think or move. She ached, the pains in her muscles like stabbing needles. Yet somehow she forced herself up on her elbow high enough to peer out the porthole. Sunlight was streaming down and the sea had calmed to a gentle roll.

She tried to move from her bed. Slow, painstaking movements allowed her to hobble past the curtain. She looked over to John's side. His bunk was empty. "John?" she called out weakly, balancing herself against the doorway.

Quick, familiar footsteps sounded across the deck. He looked down at her and smiled. "Well, some fine first mate you are. Did you get your nap out?" He was smiling and his voice was warm. He gave her a quick once-over. "Not too bad, considering."

"John," she responded in a serious tone, "how long have I been asleep?"

"A long time," he said forlornly. "Long enough for me to repair all the rigging by myself." He smiled again. "But you look as though you could stand even more rest. Why don't you lie back down and I'll get you something to eat."

"Wha-what happened?"

"You mean the storm?"

She nodded. "The last thing I remember we were both passed out."

He shook his head. "No, you were passed out. I was only . . . resting. Then I knew I had to get back to work when I heard you somewhere off in the distance talking about the sea being stronger than we were." He winked good-naturedly.

122

"You were, too, passed out," she protested. "You passed out before I did."

"Maybe so." He laughed, holding up a finger to her. "But I also came to before you did. I must have only been unconscious for a few minutes, because I did hear you. It seemed like you were a million miles away, but I heard you."

She opened her mouth to speak, but he talked on.

"Actually the storm ended shortly afterward. I've been through some squalls and some disturbances I thought were storms, but that was the worst I've ever seen. We were lucky, Kenda. Lucky."

"I know."

"Now, you crawl back into your bunk and get some more rest."

"I'd rather have something to eat. I'm going to freshen up and come up to the kitchen."

"Okay. I made a pot of stew this morning just in case."

A few minutes later, dressed in shorts and shirt, she walked into the kitchen where John had a bowl of stew waiting. Every time she thought of the storm a shudder ran through her. They had been so close to dying. Her body still ached with dull, pounding pain. She took a bite. "This is good." She tried to sound as light as he sounded.

"It'll take a day or two to regain our strength." His dark eyes played on her face.

Kenda felt the heat rise in her cheeks. "John," she began slowly, hoping the right words would fall into place. "What are we going to do?"

"About what? Are you worried about the damage?"

"No." She shook her head. "I mean about us."

"I don't know," he admitted. "What do you suggest?"

She felt vulnerable and uncertain. "You're very important to me, John. Not too many hours ago we could have died together. It made me think. What are we going to do when we reach home?"

He turned away with a frown and shrugged lamely. "I suppose we'll just have to wait and see."

"Why?" she asked bluntly. "Why can't we decide now?"

His jaw tensed. "I know you think you're in love with me, Kenda. You *think* you are, but—"

"But nothing. Nothing will ever change that fact. I am."

He moved restlessly in his chair, glanced up briefly at her, and began tapping his spoon on the table. His brow wore a deep furrow.

"Will you tell me about Lillian?" She ventured cautiously.

The furrows deepened. "What do you want to know about her?"

"Everything. Why you loved her. Why you asked her to marry you, then sailed off for months without her."

He leaned tensely back against his chair and smoothed his hair. "We were kind of thrown together, mutual friends playing matchmaker," he replied easily. "She is a beautiful woman, a brilliant woman, but"—he shrugged —"we're very different people. She's an attorney. She has her practice. I have my company. We had less and less time for each other. I don't really know her, nor does she know me." He scratched the side of his face thoughtfully. "And I don't suppose we really care that much about finding out about each other. I talked to her from Suva and she told me she felt we would never have any kind of proper marriage, whatever that meant. I agreed with her. You see, I knew this months ago, but I wanted her to draw her own conclusions. That's why I took off these months." He halted a moment, then went on. "I am a firm believer that absence does not make the heart grow fonder, not a long absence anyway." He grinned. "Maybe a few hours, or a few minutes, but not months. Particularly if the relationship is a weak one to begin with."

"Is your engagement to her broken?"

He nodded. "Yes. Unofficially when I sailed from California, officially when I called from Suva."

"Why didn't you tell me? Why have you allowed me to think you're still engaged?"

"You never asked." He looked her squarely in the eye. "If you had asked, then I would have told you."

Sensing an affront, she said cautiously, "You haven't been exactly willing to discuss your life with me. Any questions I've asked have received the most evasive answers you could come up with."

His eyes were suddenly scrutinizing her with a thoroughness that made her squirm in her chair. His gaze began at her face, moved unabashedly down her neck, and came to a halt on her breasts.

"Do you find me to be undesirable, Kenda? Is that why you wouldn't give yourself to me the other day? Or was it because you thought I was pledged to another woman? Why did you pull away from me?"

She struggled with her reply. "No, John, I certainly don't find you to be undesirable." She pulled her shoulders up. "I—I don't know how to answer that. I suppose part of it was the fact that I believed you were engaged to

Lillian. But that wasn't all of it." She held her tongue, trying to think clearly.

"Are you afraid?" he asked, his voice gentle. "Are you afraid of pain?"

A hot flush of color burned her cheeks. She said nothing.

He smiled and his eyes fastened on hers. "It will happen, you know. Somewhere between here and Hawaii, it will happen. We may have survived one kind of storm, but there's another brewing that we won't be strong enough to survive. I didn't know it earlier, but I know it now."

She moistened her lips with her tongue. For several moments she sat perfectly still, then she took another spoonful of stew. "This really is good, John."

CHAPTER TEN

Several days before crossing the equator they hit the doldrums, the wide windless belts that circle the earth. The *Beauty*'s sails, wing and wing, hung limp overhead. The rolling, gentle swells of the sea had become less than tiny ripples on a surface of mirrorlike water. It was hard for Kenda to believe that this was the same sea that had spawned a storm of such fierceness days earlier. The *Beauty* seemed to be hovering in one spot, barely moving, if at all. Perspiration gathered above her lip and she reached up and wiped it away, only to have it reappear before her hand left her face.

John sat silently on deck across from her, his bold profile silhouetted against the endless stretch of water beyond him. Wearing only blue cutoffs, he stretched out his legs and propped his arms on the railing. To ease the perspiration running down his face, he had tied a red bandanna around his head.

"John, do you have another one of those?"

He looked around to question, then saw her eyes on the bandanna. "Yes," he answered, getting up slowly. "I'll get you one." A moment later he was back holding a blue one in his hand. He walked up behind her and lowered himself into a crouching position. Folding the scarf into a thick band a bit more than an inch wide, he brought it around her head and tied it securely in the back. Finished, he brushed his hands together. "That should do it." He started to get up, then suddenly relaxed down beside her. A strange smile touched his lips, an amused smile. "I suppose it would be okay to sit close to you. In this kind of weather I'm completely trustworthy."

She smiled, her bright blue eyes considering him. "If that be the case, you won't mind if I take off my clothes, will you? I've been thinking about splashing myself."

He replied in a jovial voice, "I said I was trustworthy. My word is good. If you take yours off, I will too. Then we can splash each other."

An expression of good-natured distrust rested on her face. "I don't know if I believe you, John Taylor. You look honest. You sound honest, but—"

"Am I honest?" he finished for her with a sly grin. "There's only one way to know for sure. Want to find out?"

A look of real uncertainty flickered across Kenda's face. "Uh—I guess there's no big rush. I want some time to think about it."

John tugged at his earlobe and smiled. "All right, think about it, and while you're deep in thought, think about marrying me, will you?"

Her mouth opened in disbelief. She closed it, then it fell

open again. "Marrying you?" She blinked her eyes. "Marry?" For a moment she was struck with the thought that she had misunderstood him.

"You asked me what I wanted to do about us, remember? Now, what is it about my decision you find so disagreeable? I thought it was a rather good one myself." He chuckled warmly. "I would like to marry you, Kenda, so think about that when you do your thinking."

She sighed. "John, I don't have to think about it. I want to marry you more than anything."

Kenda's first impulse was to throw herself into John's arms, but she sat perfectly still, simply staring into the eyes of the man she loved, the man who wanted to marry her. The whole idea was too new, too strange. She thought for a moment that she had imagined the entire conversation. But there was John, crouched down beside her with that cocky, amused smile, making his eyes dance with light. No, she hadn't imagined it all. It was true, too good to be true.

"Can we be married in Hawaii or California?" she questioned softly. "Which did you have in mind?" Now the joyful words rushed out. "It won't matter to me, either place. It doesn't matter to me."

He reached for her hand, carefully turning it in his. "To be truthful, Kenda, I would prefer to marry you here—now. If you want to wait until we reach port, that will be fine, I suppose, but for myself I would prefer the *Beauty* —now."

"How can we do that?" she asked in amazement. "There's no way we can, is there?"

"Yes." Thoughtfully he scratched his face again. "I'm the captain of the ship *Beauty*. I can in that capacity perform marriages. I don't know how some people might view it, but to me it would be legal and binding. I want to marry you, Kenda. I realized it during the storm. I don't know why it takes near disaster sometimes for people to realize what is truly important in their lives, but I realized during all those long hours I fought to keep the *Beauty* from breaking up how important you have become to my life. That's when I first thought of marrying you. I thought about it hour after hour while the sea threw all she had at me. Hardly a second passed when I didn't think of you."

"Why didn't you tell me before now?" She ran her fingers along the top of his hand. "That was days ago, John. Why didn't you tell me then?"

"There were some things I still needed to think out," he replied in little more than a whisper.

"And have you?"

He nodded. "I think so." Suddenly he was cheerful again. "Anyway, I waited until we hit the doldrums. I figured if a marriage could survive this, it can survive anything."

Hardly a second passed before she found herself in his arms. His lips briefly touched her cheek.

"What do you think about, say, sunrise tomorrow morning?" he whispered in her ear. "We'll pledge our vows, and who knows, maybe live happily ever after."

A quick nod of her head answered him.

"Now," he chuckled, "what about our splashing?"

"I think we had better wait until tomorrow for that too." She laughed. "To be truthful, I don't trust you."

A small gust of wind swept astern. The sails billowed out above it and stirred the *Beauty* across a few feet of water before the wind ceased and the canvas sails again fell limp. Kenda wiped the perspiration from her face, fighting to keep her outpouring of emotions from billowing out like the sails.

Suddenly John jumped up and grabbed her hand, pulling her after him. "Let's prepare a wedding feast!" he exclaimed happily. "The works. We'll spare no expense. I'll make a cake, even bake you a loaf of my famous saltwater bread. You can take charge of the vegetables and fruit, and tonight I'll catch our fish for the main course."

Later that night, unable to sleep from the excitement intermingled with the heat, Kenda slipped quietly up on deck and sat down, looking up at the star-filled sky. In the silent stillness she was overwhelmed with the breathtaking splendor of it all. John wanted to marry her. That made the soft, rhythmic creaking of the boat, the light from the *Beauty* that drifted over the surface of the deep blue sea, the bright moonlit night—the fact that John wanted to marry her made it all more perfect.

She heard him tiptoeing behind her. Then his arms came around her and he pulled her back close to him. "What are you doing?" he asked. "Have you changed your mind?"

"No, I'll never change my mind," she said, and kissed his arm. "I just feel too wonderful to sleep. It's like I don't want to lose a precious moment. I want to remember it all."

"Kenda?" His voice was low and serious. "I want to tell you about Barbara and"—he swallowed—"and Jill."

Her spirits lifted even higher. The last secrets were slipping away. With a wave of happiness she turned in arms and looked up at his muscular physique, the handsomeness of his face. Then she realized how very serious his features were. "Tell me," she whispered.

He met her gaze directly. "Barbara and I were married when we were both still in college. I was a senior, she a sophomore. We were very much in love." He paused and stirred. "Three years later we weren't. I don't know what you blame it on when you don't love someone anymore. Maybe youth. Our families were against the marriage. We were warned, but we were headstrong. Anyway, when our passion for each other died—and that happened over a remarkably short period—we decided to separate. We were separated for over a year, then circumstances brought us back together and we decided to make another attempt at it. We didn't make it that time either, and when she left, she told me she would be getting a divorce." He shook his head. "We both agreed and she had already filed when she found out she was pregnant. After some lengthy discussions we decided to hold off on the divorce, at least until the baby was born. But we never lived together as man and wife from that time." His voice was barely a whisper. "Jill was born, and she was the most beautiful little baby girl you could imagine."

Kenda smiled. She could well imagine that. It was easy to believe that his child was beautiful.

"But she was not born healthy. She had numerous heart defects. It was hard to believe that such a little baby could have so much wrong with her—valve defects, even a couple of the heart vessels were transposed. From the day she was born she required continuous medical treatment. During the first few months of her life she underwent open heart surgery three times." His brows drew together. "I was trying to build my business; my father had financed me and I didn't want him to lose his money, so I split my life between my company and my daughter." He sighed heavily. "Barbara existed somewhere in the background during those years. She didn't love me, I didn't love her, but we both loved Jill. We stayed together another six years that way. My third year in business showed a profit of three-quarters of a million dollars, and from that point on I've been fortunate. We were able to provide Jill with the best medical attention in the world. I flew her to Houston, South Africa, and finally to Boston, where she had her last surgery. She had already survived six years with a heart that had been hopeless from birth." He shook his head slowly. "Then, for the first time, for the very first time in all those years, we were given the first ray of hope. All the valves had been corrected. A team of surgeons told us that if the vessels could be rerouted, Jill might be allowed to lead a somewhat normal life. Barbara was against the surgery, adamantly opposed to it. We had a terrible argument."

"Why?" Kenda asked with anxious concern. "Why would she oppose it?"

"Because of the risk involved. The technique had been both successful and unsuccessful." He glanced away from Kenda now. "Jill wanted so much from life. She hated not being able to run and play. She wanted more than anything to sail with me on the *Beauty*. And I suppose I wanted it as badly as she did. I would sit for hours in the evening and read to her. Sometimes we would go down to the harbor, just the two of us, and spend the night on the *Beauty* while she lay anchored." His dark eyes began to glisten in the darkness. "It took some doing, but between Jill and me we finally convinced Barbara to agree to the operation." He swallowed hard. "She died on the operating table in Boston. She died." Now the tears spilled over and traveled a path along his face.

Kenda reached across and, with a soft touch of her fingertips, wiped them away. Then she reached up and brushed her own away.

"I couldn't believe it," he went on. "I never thought about her dying, not once. Not even knowing the many risks involved, I just never thought about it. It's been over four years and sometimes even now I still can't believe it."

"That's what you meant that day when you told me you had planned for your family to sail with you, but you sailed alone."

He nodded. "Yes. You see, I had a family one day and the next day I didn't. I can't tell you the guilt I felt, Kenda. It was so overpowering it almost destroyed me. I knew Barbara blamed me for Jill's death, and I blamed myself. It took that year alone for me to understand that I didn't kill my little girl. Nobody killed her. It was nobody's fault she died." He attempted a bleak smile and whispered, "All the fine surgeons, and all the king's men, just couldn't help my little girl."

Releasing a sigh, Kenda put her head on his shoulder. She didn't try to speak. There were no words that could relay her emotions at that moment.

Abruptly he cleared his throat. "And Barbara, well, Barbara picked up the pieces of her life and fit them back together. Two years ago she married an insurance broker from London and she now lives there. I received a card from her at Christmas, the first time I've heard from her since our divorce. The card sounded happy. I suppose she is. I hope she is."

"So do I," Kenda murmured softly. "So do I."

"I wanted you to know," he confided, then continued with noticeable sadness in his voice, "in case it should have some bearing on our plans. I wanted you to know."

Lifting her head from his shoulder, she gazed into his solemn face. "I can't fight a memory, John. I don't want to. You have your memories, and I have mine. I want us to share them with each other," the words tumbled from her lips. "I used to be so lonely for someone just to talk with. I was starved for the sound of another human voice, but after a while I came to accept my aloneness. And then, when I had given up all hope of ever hearing another human voice, you came—and I heard yours. I will never forget the expression on your face when I turned around and saw you behind me." She smiled. "There you were, the answer to all my prayers, all of them." She blinked back tears. "I already have a thousand memories of you, and nothing will ever separate them from me. You have a thousand memories of your dau . . . Jill, and I have no desire to separate them from you. If anything, I love you more for it."

He caught her hands in his and held them close to his heart. A long silence followed, until she finally whispered, "I think I'll go below." As she started down to the cabin, she heard him removing the fishing gear behind her.

In the ensuing hours she could not close her eyes. She tossed and turned restlessly, her heart twisting in heartbreak for him. Sitting up in bed, she opened the porthole and a warm westerly breeze sifted in slowly. She inhaled it deeply. Tonight's conversation disturbed her as none other had. Surprised. Shocked. Saddened. She was all those and more. But some good had come from the night.

All the tensions between them were eased. She and John would have the rest of their lives together without dark secrets lurking in the background threatening at any moment to bring disaster to a happy marriage.

She was determined their marriage would be happy. This awareness began to fill her with excitement. She had not expected his proposal of marriage, even knowing how much she loved him and wanted him in her life always. The past weeks with him had told her that there could never be another man for her. There would only be John. Tonight. Tomorrow. And always.

Feeling happy again, she smiled in the darkness. He had tried to be indifferent to her. He had fought his own personal battle and lost. In his losing she had won. She sighed softly. There had been times in the past few weeks when she felt the wounds from his battle, but all wounds had healed tonight.

She looked at the heavy canvas curtain that had separated them for the past weeks. Trembling, she reached out and touched it. Today had been the last day it would divide the private lives of two people. Something profound stirred in her heart and she felt a powerful emotion move in her.

Feeling a trifle restless, she decided to take another quiet stroll on deck, for she was not yet comfortable with all her thoughts. She had not heard John come down to bed, so she felt she would probably find him exactly where she had left him. Fishing.

Instead, she found him staring out into the darkness, smoking a cigarette. "Did you have any luck?" she asked lightly, sitting down beside him.

"Of course." A giant smile arched his lips. "A beauty."

Kenda cast a quick glance at his face and found it wearing a mysterious expression in the flickering light of the lantern. She wondered what his thoughts must be like: if perhaps he was sorry he had proposed marriage, if he regretted it and would now like to change his mind.

Almost as if he could read her thoughts, he said softly, "I suppose in moments like these, Kenda, men and women aren't too different. You can't sleep. I can't sleep. It's a mixture of excitement, fear, happiness, and doubt. Perhaps more excitement and happiness, but neither of us can deny that the fear and doubt are also there."

"Yes, I know." She dropped her gaze from his face and began fingering the sash to her robe. "I am a bit frightened. I don't know why. I want to marry you, John. I love you. I have no doubts there. I feel I am the luckiest woman in the world."

"And I, the luckiest man," he murmured, blowing smoke into the still air around them. "When it seemed there was no one in this world for me to truly share my life and dreams with, I found you. You said earlier tonight that you were starved for the sound of another human voice, and in my own way I have been starved too, not for voices, but for someone to wrap my arms around and say 'I love you, I love you,' and not only say it, for those are the three easiest, most misused words in our language, but say it and know from the depth of my heart that I meant it. Many times I have wondered if I ever would."

"I am waiting to hear them, John. Those three easiest, most misused words in our language . . . I have been waiting from that day we met to hear them."

In the lantern light his eyes had a gold and piercing quality as they met hers. "I do love you," he said simply.

"Very much." Then his hand moved and his fingers softly touched her chin. "And I want you to know, that whatever happens, I will always love you."

"Why—why do you say that?" She looked at him with troubled, uncertain eyes. "Whatev happens?"

"So much lies ahead." He shrugged. "So much."

"Let's face it then," she murmured. "Not tonight, or tomorrow, let's face it when it happens." Her voice was steady, her emotions shaking. What did he fear so? What could be ahead of the two of them that made him think of their future as some kind of gray cloud? Oh, God, she so loved him. "John?" she asked in a low voice. "In the morning, tell me, how will it be? The wedding."

He raised his brows slightly. "You mean the actual ceremony?"

She nodded. "Yes, how will it be, since you're both the captain and the groom?"

He gave a soft laugh.

"What are you laughing about?"

"That sounded strange. I am both the captain and the groom." He ran a finger down the line of her cheekbone to her chin, then up to her lips. He suddenly bent his head and kissed her startled mouth, then quickly pulled away from her. "Say what is in your heart tomorrow." His murmur was explicit. "I will." He rose slowly to his feet. "I have work to do. The fish won't clean itself, or cook itself. I don't want to spend any of our day tomorrow in the everyday chores of staying afloat."

Though she didn't want to leave him, she didn't protest. "Can I help?"

He smiled back at her. "I thought you'd never ask."

She followed him to the kitchen, where he began preparing the fish to bake. "John?" she asked, watching him clean the fish. "Will I live in Los Angeles with you?"

"Of course." He did not look up from his task.

"What will I do there?"

He cut his eyes quickly to her. "Be my wife."

They laughed in unison. Those words were worth more than a billion dollars to her. Oh, Lord, how well it had worked out. Now she wouldn't have to use the plan she had perfected in her mind just to stay near him. Now she could tell him. "I had wanted to go to Los Angeles with you. Did you suspect that? I was going to ask you to take me with you so that I could finish my education, but mainly so that I could be near you."

With his back to her, he turned on the oven. Taking the fish, he placed in on aluminum foil, seasoned it, then folded the foil neatly in a tight seal. After placing it in the gas oven, he washed his hands, dried them, and then slowly turned to her, his body tense.

"Did you hear me?" she asked, smiling. "I already had my plans never to leave you."

"Yes, I heard," he said almost curtly. "But I doubt that arrangement would have worked out."

"Why not?" she inquired, her eyes wide. "I need to finish my education, don't you think?" She could feel the quickening of her pulse, the sudden upheaval deep inside her.

He relaxed and smiled. "Are we going to talk about school the night before our wedding? Darling, those are matters we can take care of weeks from now. You'll be mine, Kenda. I'll take care of you, so don't worry your beautiful head with needless thoughts." He reached for her hand and their eyes met and held. "For now, let's just look forward to the sunrise."

"I do look forward to the sunrise," she murmured, her fingers clutching his. "May it be the most beautiful sunrise of our lives."

He reached into his pocket for another cigarette. "Why don't you try to sleep awhile. I'm going to turn in in a few minutes myself."

In her bed, moments later, she looked out over the horizon to the cluster of stars and the moon casting silvery lines across the water. She sat with her arms about her updrawn knees watching for the first streak of light. And when it came, she spoke a silent prayer.

CHAPTER ELEVEN

It was a glorious morning, a sunrise to dream about, to tuck away in the portion of the heart reserved for memories, to bring out again and relive over and over in the days to come. Kenda hesitated about what to wear. She heard John rummaging through his drawers. "John?" she questioned softly. "Do you want me to wear my dress?"

"No. Be comfortable. If we dress in our finery, we'll both probably perish before midmorning."

She smiled. Pulling on her white shorts set, all her thoughts and all her courage were focused on the sunrise. She slid her feet into her sandals, then reached for the blue bandanna and tied it around her head. She was at least wearing the traditional colors. "John," she called out. "I need something old."

"You're getting me. Will that do?" He laughed. Seconds later he passed a gold chain behind the curtain.

"Here, this is old. My mother gave it to me when I graduated from high school. Want me to put it on for you?"

"No, I'll manage." She took the chain from his hand and placed it around her neck, then fastened it. "What will your family say about this?" she asked after a few seconds.

"They'll think at last I've finally done something smart." Again he laughed. "They'll love you." He paused. "I'm going on deck. See you in a few minutes."

Minutes later she came up on deck and walked forward to where he stood next to the railing. She smiled, and white teeth flashed between her full red lips, her cheeks flushed pink with excitement.

He wore clean, pressed khaki shorts and a white short-sleeved shirt. Tied around his head was a red bandanna. "Good morning," he said simply, then leaned forward and kissed her. "I love you."

"And I love you," she whispered in return.

There was the faintest hint of a breeze blowing as they turned their eyes to the east where the sun slowly etched its way up from behind the still, blue water, casting a bright chain of light across the horizon. His hand reached down and clutched hers tightly. In his right hand he held a worn Bible. "Shall we?" he asked in a whisper.

Slowly she nodded.

Taking the Bible in both hands, he held it so that she might place hers on top, resting against his. His voice came low and soft, "Kenda, I love you." He stepped closer, close enough that she could feel the breath from his words on her face. "I want all that is good for you, both in this world and in the hereafter. I will do all in my power to make you happy, so that we may live our lives in such a way that we leave the world a better place for having

142

lived at all." He cleared his throat and continued huskily. "Knowing you has given direction to my floundering life. Loving you has given me new purpose for existence. Marrying you charts a new course for my future. I love you. I need you. I will take care of you for however long I may live." He inhaled deeply. "With God as our lone witness, I pledge my heart to you forever." He lapsed into silence, his eyes shining with love.

She smiled at him enchantingly as she edged her hands atop the Bible to rest on his. Her heart had lifted higher than the clear blue sky overhead. For a brief moment she struggled with tears, but then fought them away successfully. There would be no tears this day. Her words came only a tinge above a whisper. "I will never believe other than one day God looked down from His Heaven and saw me alone on a forsaken island of paradise. He had pity for me so He searched the whole world over for someone to come for me so that I might know what it is to truly be alive. He sent you to me, John." Her face became radiant with happiness as she paused for breath. "I will not deny that I loved you from the very first moment I saw you. I did. I saw in your face courage and integrity; I saw in your eyes a sadness for things past; I saw in your arms—heaven. Today is ours. This sunrise will be ours for always and there will be no one on this earth who can ever dim the glow of this moment. I love you, John Taylor. May these words we have spoken to each other as we exchange our vows of marriage be forever present in our memories, intact, never to be forgotten. May the love we feel for each other accompany us from this moment, throughout eternity. May God in His Heaven smile and say, 'I did one of my best days' work the day I sent John Taylor and

Beauty to My forsaken paradise in the South Pacific, for it wasn't forsaken—only waiting." Her lips touched his cheek. "I pledge my love to you with these vows of marriage, with God as our lone witness." She again kissed his cheek, then drew back a single step and smiled. Her golden hair reflected the glow of the sunrise, her eyes shone blue as the water about them as she looked at him.

His gaze met hers with a tenderness as deep as the shimmering sea. As he reached out and drew her against him, his mouth touched hers gently and he breathed into her mouth, "Hello, Kenda Vaughn Taylor. I love you." His hands were warm on her waist as he gazed down at her for a long moment. "What do you say to a celebration?"

She laughed and her teeth flashed white in the now bright sunlight. "I'm ready, but we aren't going to eat fish at this time of day, are we?"

"No, not fish, but we're going to toast our marriage." He kissed her again.

"With what?" she murmured, not wanting to be freed from his embrace.

He pulled away and hurried down the steps to the cabin, seconds later returning carrying a bottle and dragging the canvas curtain behind him. He waved the bottle at her. "Come help me," he called.

She ran over and took the bottle from his hand. She looked at it in amazement. "Where did you get this?" She read the label. "Champagne."

led aloud. His hands were busily folding the had divided the cabin throughout the voyain worth his salt is always prepared for celebrations." He nodded at her. "Why

144

don't you get us glasses, unless you want to drink from the bottle."

"Let's do that," she replied giddily. "Let's drink from the bottle."

"Fine." He agreed and placed the folded canvas in the storage box near the mainsail. Straightening, he brushed his hands. "So much for our canvas chaperone." He grinned wickedly as he lifted the bottle from her hands. He took his knife from his pocket and began to work the cork. A second later, a pop, then a quick spew. "I've had it in the freezer since before daybreak, but it may still be a little warm," he said apologetically, holding the bottle out for her.

She took it and turned it up to her mouth.

"Wait a minute." His hand caught her arm. "We didn't toast yet."

"Sorry," she said, grinning at him. "I've never tasted champagne. I suppose I'm overanxious."

"Don't be." His hand folded about hers. "There's a lot of things you've never done. Don't be overanxious, just ride with the tide, my little darling. Now"—he nudged her knee with his—"let's toast. Here's to happiness." With his hands around hers, he lifted the bottle to her lips, then it went to his. They swallowed. "Your turn," he said.

"Here's to love and marriage." Again they drank.

"Here's to a long life of calm seas."

She smiled when he nodded to her. "And here's to our children . . . and our children's children."

For a brief moment a sad memory flickered in his eyes, then disappeared. "Yes," he whispered, "to our children." They drank the toast, then he took the bottle and set it on deck. "That's enough," he stated firmly. "Too many toasts

145

with warm champagne on a hot day will inebriate the bride and groom, and the groom doesn't want that to happen."

"Neither does the bride," she giggled. Already the bubbles were traveling throughout her body, encountering no obstacles through her empty stomach.

His eyes carefully weighed her reaction to the drink and a few minutes later she found herself seated at the table with a plate of scrambled eggs and bacon in front of her. "This isn't our feast," she reminded him somewhat thick-tongued.

"No," he agreed, "it isn't. The feast will come later, but for now eat your breakfast, drink you coffee, and take your salt pills there beside your plate."

She grinned at him, seeing the tiny beads of perspiration on his face. "If I do, can we splash after breakfast?" She leaned across, staring wide-eyed.

He laughed and nodded. "Yes, if you'll do all that, we'll splash after breakfast." His eyes flickered over her hair and face, then swept down across her body.

She didn't know whether it was the champagne or the expression on his face that made her heart beat so madly she suddenly felt dizzy and off balance. What heavenly moments, she thought to herself. What heavenly . . . heavenly moments. She felt like a princess in a newly found kingdom. She turned her attention to the plate of food, unable to endure John's eyes, that had set off a reaction in her of such excitement it was smothering her appetite for food. She tried to clean her plate, but could only manage to choke down half. She did, however, empty the cup of hot coffee. "I'm finished," she said in a small voice.

As if by an unspoken understanding between them,

both rose slowly from the chairs and went into the cabin. Kenda stood in the middle of the room and looked around. "It's so much larger than it seemed with that curtain," she said in amazement.

He made no reply. His eyes had not left her face.

Taking a towel from her drawer, Kenda went into the bathroom. After washing herself she wrapped the towel around her. When she opened the door to the cabin, she saw John sitting on his bed with a towel wrapped around his waist. For the first time in her life she didn't think her knees would carry her from the spot she stood. A force so strong took complete control of her mind that nothing mattered beyond the desire to be crushed to every inch of his male body. He extended his hand to her, and when fingertips touched, it was like touching fire. She stood both rigid and trembling.

He smiled at her. The portholes on both sides of the room were open and the bright sunlight sifted in, stirred by a warm air carrying with it the clean fragrance of the sea that surrounded them.

Kenda touched her towel nervously. She could sense the heat from his body shimmering in the small distance that separated them. Hardly breathing, she felt her heart thumping wildly within her chest. Then she felt the strong grip of his hands on her arms and as her lips parted to utter a cry, she felt his hot, firm mouth on hers. Instantly arms of iron encircled her and she sank to the bed in his embrace as his tongue shot between her lips. She felt his hand on her back as he lifted the towel away from ~ body and it fell to the floor. Then she felt his own slip away and she gasped.

"What is it, darling?" his murmur came thick with emotion. His kisses softened. "Are you frightened?"

She nodded. "A little," she whispered in reply.

He pulled away from her ever so slightly and smiled while his embrace of iron slowly melted. Then he sat up and flexed his shoulders. "Let's go up on deck and splash," he said softly.

"John." She laid her head next to his. "Let's don't. I'm not frightened of you. I love you. It's these overwhelming feelings that are both wonderful and terrifying, feelings that take my breath away. Do you understand? It isn't you. I love you."

He kept his tone low and soft. "There's plenty of time, darling, we don't have to—"

Her fingers went to his lips and stopped his flow of words midsentence. "We hope there's plenty of time." Her mouth was brushing his ear. "But we know there's now."

"You are so remarkably beautiful, my darling," he said quietly. "You can't imagine how you look to me." He kissed her mouth again and her lips parted as she returned his kiss.

"And you are beautiful to me," she whispered, drawing back from his lips a breath. "Perfect for a fact." Then she sighed as the warm sensation spread throughout her like the tiny champagne bubbles had done earlier in the morning, leaving her tipsy and light-headed.

He chuckled low. "Now, what do you know about perfect men?" His lips crushed hers.

She knew about one perfect, beautiful man. He was beautiful—broad, muscular shoulders; narrow, firm waist; slight hips; strong, muscular legs with hair bleached white from the sun. She knew about beautiful men and perfect men. She was in the arms of one.

His fingertips lightly caressed her shoulders, her neck, her ears, then pressed a hot path to her breasts. She felt a soft moan escape her lips.

Suddenly he released her and took her face gently in his hands. He kissed her lightly, then whispered in breathless desire. "If only we could keep this moment forever." His lips then met hers, at last free of all restraints, and as their bodies coiled together, she sank on the bed in his embrace.

Whatever fears of the unknown she had, disappeared beneath the roaring of the joyous drums pounding in her head, drumming out all other sounds in the whole universe. Everything was forgotten except the feel of his body upon hers, the soft touch of his hair against her cheek. His hands were everywhere on her flesh, everywhere . . . touching . . . probing.

"Kenda," he murmured, his lips hovering on hers. "Please tell me if I hurt you."

"You aren't, darling, believe me, you aren't." She had reached a new plateau of existence, feelings she could not quiet or deny, a bliss that kept climbing higher and higher. Her arms were tight around him, her fingers buried in his hair at the base of his neck. His lips demanded more, more of her.

She uttered a sharp cry and the burning pain in her loins swiftly subsided as the sense of fullness grew within and the world began to rise and fall around her like the endless sea outside. She was no longer one flesh; her flesh had fused with his and in doing so she glimpsed all secrets of life and love, for they had penetrated the depths of each other's souls.

He swept her on and on in the newfound world of ecstasy until finally all that existed were fiery lights, the fire and the shuddering that transported her into a whirling land of sensation beyond description. It seemed she would never catch her breath.

He drew her to him and held her tight in his arms, his damp hair touching her face. They lay not moving for a while, his hands tracing her back slowly, brushing the curves of her hips, his eyes scanning her face.

Still breathless, she lay with her eyes closed, listening to the sounds of his breathing.

"I love you," he said finally.

She peered at him and smiled. "I love you." She slid her arms around his neck and brought his lips to hers. "I love you," she repeated in a murmur.

It was late afternoon when John took Kenda's hand and led her up on deck. "Now comes splash time," he said with a laugh, reaching for the pail. "Should refresh us before dinner."

The water was cool to her parched skin as he splashed her again and again. "It feels marvelous," she sighed as the streams ran down her body and onto the deck. After a few minutes he handed her the pail. She doused him once, then began to laugh.

"What's so funny, if it's not impertinent for me to ask?"

"Your butt. It's so white compared to the rest of your body."

He reddened. "Well, I suppose that's because I haven't run around naked for half my life."

Filling the bucket, she emptied it over the top of his head slowly, and watched it travel down his body. "Why don't we not dress the next few days," she suggested with a smile. "Then it can tan like the rest of you. Wouldn't that be nice?"

He thought a moment then said, "I suppose so, but I don't know if I'd be comfortable running around all day without anything on. I doubt that I'm as uninhibited as you."

She began to apply the lotion to his back. Already the day was ending. Looking past him to the golden streaks of the sunset, she said, "It's been a beautiful day."

"Yes," he replied. "The most beautiful of my life."

A proud smile broke across her face. "Do you mean it, John? The *most*?"

He turned around and took her in his arms. "Yes, I mean it. This day has added a new dimension to my life."

She brushed the wet hair off his forehead. "I can hardly remember life before you, and I can't imagine what it would be like without you. You are my life, John. You're my world."

That night, after spreading dinner on deck and eating a hearty meal of fish, saltwater bread, baked potatoes, and fruit salad, they cut the cake John had made the night before. The sea around them lay motionless and the stillness that surrounded them was absolute and heightened their quiet mood of contentment.

John wiped a piece of cake from the corner of his mouth. "I checked our progress and we've come only thirty miles today. At this rate my butt will be as tan as the rest of my body before we leave the doldrums." He grinned at her and placed a bite of cake in her mouth. "However, if I should get a sunburn on certain parts of my anatomy, I will naturally do what all good husbands do, I will put the blame on you."

"You won't," she replied knowingly, "get a sunburn, that is."

He laughed. "You would make a good poker player, did you know that, my darling? You sound so authoritative about subjects I know you don't know anything about. In case you didn't notice, our anatomies are somewhat different."

"I noticed." She laughed, then paused. "You have small breasts."

That night as she lay snug in his arms, Kenda had never felt as secure in her life. She snuggled closer to him and, with her hand over his heart, felt it beating, and, feeling the wonderful sensation against her hand, drifted off to sleep.

When she awoke the next morning, he was sitting flat on the floor beside the bed looking at her. Seeing her open her eyes he smiled.

She reached out for him.

He took her hand, got up from the floor, and climbed in beside her, pulling her close.

She responded eagerly to his touch, matching his kisses, running her hands along his body until she was on her back and he was on top of her. It was silent and beautiful, and at the highest point, he whispered in her ear, "Good morning, darling."

CHAPTER TWELVE

Ten days following the wedding the *Beauty* traveled beyond the stretch of calm seas and suddenly there was the usual activity of full-scale sailing and rolling swells and whipping spray. Kenda no longer feared the voyage's end, for there would not be the good-bye and the distance of the ocean between Honolulu and Los Angeles to keep them apart. The future now looked so wildly beautiful and exciting, she welcomed it. She had not known before entering the windless belts that surrounded the earth that when she left them she would be the wife of John Taylor.

In the lovely days that followed the ceremony she had come to know the other side of John's nature, the side he had kept hidden from her. She learned through his talks how thoroughly educated he was in the world of business. He seemed to know all there was to know about architecture and construction. He was also very cultured, displaying a tremendous amount of knowledge of the various arts—music, literature, theater. He seemed quite happy and content to discuss the life he lived on land.

Then came the times when nothing else existed, no other worlds for either of them except the wonderful world of each other's bodies, a dissolving world of passions until both were spent and lay clinging to each other. She loved him and now she knew he loved her, and the two loves combined were more beautiful than anything she could have ever imagined.

Every night after dinner, in the romantic flicker of the deck lantern, they would spend leisurely hours talking and laughing, sometimes with a cup of coffee if the night winds were cold. Kenda didn't mind the cold; she liked bundling up next to her husband while the brisk wind blew against her cheeks. At nights sometimes after he had gone to sleep she would lie awake in the narrow bed and relive every moment of the day just past, every word, ever fleeting smile, every laugh.

It was well into the afternoon of the fourteenth day of being Mrs. John Taylor when Kenda asked, "Do you still plan for us to stop by Fanning Island for a few days, John? If the maps and charts and compass are right, we should be there in the next day or so."

He nodded. "I think a few days on land will do us good. I have some friends on the island." His eyes fastened on the sky. "Trouble is I don't know what kind of weather is in the making. The sky looks hazy, strange. But maybe we'll be on land by the time we find out what's brewing."

She smiled shakily. "You don't think it's another storm, do you? Heavens, I don't think I could stand another one like the last one." She shivered with the terrible thought.

Even the slightest prospect of another storm—she shook her head—she couldn't think about it.

He shot her a quizzical look. "Kenda, I don't believe it's a storm. Maybe some rain and mist. I had the radio on a few minutes ago and the weather report from Christmas Island didn't relay any severe weather warnings. Besides, I don't want you to become frightened of the sea just because we had a bad experience."

"Nothing frightens you, does it, John?"

"You think not?" His eyes darkened in the deepening light of dusk. "Do you want me to tell you something?"

"Yes, tell me. What, if anything, frightens you?" Her curiosity was aroused.

"All right, my lady, I'll tell you what frightens me." While he talked he held the fishing basket eye level and examined it with a keen look, then placed the bait inside and lowered it over the rail. "Honolulu frightens me. The thought of sharing you frightens me."

"But why?" She couldn't hide the surprise in her voice. He smiled briefly. "I can't expect you to understand."

"All the same I'd like to try." She caught his arm.

There in the fading hazy light of day's end they looked at each other and she could feel his potent, overpowering attraction melting her insides.

"I'll try," he agreed, then broke off into a short silence. "You do realize, Kenda, that there will be those who will believe I took advantage of you. You had been isolated for so long with no contact with other human beings, that you would have most probably fallen in love with any man who rescued you from that island. You can't be expected to think and react like someone who has lived the past seven years in a modern society; taking your place among

155

the young women of the world will be difficult. Your milieu has been completely different from the typical environment of today's young woman. And I have probably complicated the process of your reentry into the civilized world by stealing your emotions and your love, and your virginity."

Kenda gazed up at him with bewildered eyes. "Surely you don't believe what you're saying, John. How can you believe that you have stolen what I have given to you freely?"

He said nothing in reply. Turning away from her, he began to work with the rigging of the mainsail.

She watched him a few seconds, then went down and began cleaning the cabin. Oh, Lord, surely he wasn't going to allow doubts or fears of what other people thought and said to enter into their blissful world. He had married her, made love to her, known what it was like to become the man in her life, and now, how could he have doubts! She saw the need to fight his fears, but how could she manage to do that for him? That was something he would have to do within himself. Fate had cast them together on this sea. How senseless it was to say *if*. *If another had found her.* It hadn't been another—it had been John.

She straightened the sheets out carefully, then swept and scrubbed the floors. Then she went into the kitchen and set about preparing a dinner of biscuits, beans, and fruit. If he brought in a fish, she would fry it, if not, they would have to make do with what she had cooked.

Before the biscuits were done, John brought in the fish and laid it in the sink. "I cleaned it on deck," he muttered. "Want me to cook it?"

She shook her head. "No." That was all. A simple *no.*

He started out, then swung around in the doorway. "I didn't think you would understand." He grated his words. "That's why I wasn't particularly anxious to discuss it with you. The main thing that concerns me, Kenda, is one day you'll look back with regrets."

She was shocked by those words, and suddenly felt her temper flare. "Is that what you think, John Taylor!" She wanted to say something that would sting him the way his words had stung her. "Maybe it won't be one day. Maybe it'll be a lot sooner than that!"

He stomped out of the kitchen and she could hear his feet on deck pounding the floor furiously.

She slung the skillet on the gas burner and slapped the fish in it, pieces hanging over both sides. *Oh, damn . . . damn. Why did a silly argument have to happen?* With a fork she tried to push the fish in its entirety down into the skillet, and when it wouldn't fit she threw the fork into the sink and sank down in a chair.

An hour later John joined her, his lips shaped into a full pout. When she held out his plate, he accepted it with a grunt of thanks. Without a word they settled down to eat. He took a few bites.

"The biscuits are burned, the fish is raw, and I don't know what in God's name you've done to the beans, but otherwise your meal is delicious." One side of his mouth smiled and his cool gaze began to warm.

"I'm sorry." With a sigh Kenda threw down her fork. "I couldn't concentrate on cooking; other matters were pressing hard on my mind. Much more important matters."

Now his teeth bared white at her. "Is this our first quarrel?"

"Not our—your." She spoke emphatically. She still wouldn't look at his face for any length of time, just a quick glance from the top of her eyes. Then suddenly she laughed because she couldn't stop herself.

He chewed a moment on his bottom lip. "Think I'm funny, do you?"

She felt a sudden quickening of her pulse, an awareness of the expression in his dark eyes. "Yes," she breathed. "I think you're funny."

In an instant he had a hold of her wrist. "Come here. We'll see how funny I am." As he spoke he dragged her around the table and pulled her down on his lap. His hand slid under her shirt and he pulled her close to him, then brought her lips down to his in a long, unrelenting kiss. He pulled away and asked, "Now, am I funny?"

Again she nodded, and hard, hungry lips searched her face, her neck. His hands roamed her back, her breasts. He suddenly lifted her and carried her from the kitchen into the cabin and dropped her on the bed. His eyes swept her up and down. "One last chance, am I—"

"You're the funniest man I ever met," she said huskily and held her arms up to him.

The next day the northward wind was whipping strong and the *Beauty* sailed downwind toward Fanning Island. Kenda and John awakened to a dull sunlight, and by dusk, the wind had changed direction and a heavy fog descended in such thickness that the top of the mast disappeared in the whirling gray matter.

"I prefer storms to fog," John said concerned.

"I prefer sunshine," Kenda said. She was appalled by the thick covering that had settled on them. It looked as though she could reach out and brush it away with her hand. She hoped it would not last long, for it was a strange sensation to be unable to see the boat's bow or mast. She gave a last rueful glance at the fog, then went inside where John was turning the radio antenna. She heard a loud blip noise every few seconds on the receiver. "What is that?" she asked.

He was looking at the receiver when he answered, "Radio beacons, probably from Fanning. Makes it possible for aircraft to fly through fog." He set his eyes on her. "You need to get your safety harness on, and would you bring me mine." He spoke quietly but firmly.

A moment later, both in life jackets and harnesses, they sat close together leaning against the cabin wall. Kenda felt for John's hand and clutched it tightly. Everything was completely invisible now, even his face was a blur.

He patted her hand with a gentleness, saying, "Why don't you go down and try to sleep. When you wake in the morning, this should be gone."

"Are you coming to bed?"

"No. I'll stay here till it begins to clear, then I may try to get some sleep."

"I'd rather stay with you."

He leaned across and kissed her lips lightly. "And I'd feel better if you were in a place where you could see your nose. Go on now, follow the captain's orders."

"Will you kiss me again?"

"I'll come down and kiss you good night, how about that?"

"Okay, I'll be waiting."

A few minutes later, when he came down and kissed her, she looked up to him. "We have foul luck, don't we?

First that dreadful storm, and now this terrible fog. What do you think your wonderful sea will throw at us next?"

He gave a bleak laugh. "Nothing we can't handle, hopefully." He blew her a kiss from the doorway. "Now, go to sleep. Everything will be fine by morning."

She propped herself on her elbow and watched his legs disappear up the stairs. A real loneliness began to clutch her. She reached up and pulled the drape over the porthole to close off the absolute darkness outside the *Beauty*.

She wasn't sleepy. She was anything but sleepy. She thought about John up on the dark deck by himself and that made her feel even lonelier. She knew she couldn't fall asleep; there was no way she could sleep down here alone with him up there.

Maybe I'll read, she thought. Her books had saved her from the devouring loneliness on the island. She thought of every one of them as a wonderful friend. She leaned over the end of the bed and picked up the one on top. Carefully she thumbed through the weatherbeaten pages. She smiled. She had read it so many times over the years, it held no surprises between the pages.

She sat up on the edge of her bed and stroked the book for a moment, then put it back on the stack at the end of her bunk. Her eyes had glimpsed the ship's logbook on John's dresser. She was tempted. But what was it he had said: "To read the ship's log without the captain's permission is like reading someone's diary." She put the idea out of her mind and crawled under her top sheet. She twisted and turned. It was impossible to get in a comfortable position wearing clothes and the burdensome life jacket and harness. Still, she tried to lie quietly with her eyes closed and drift off to sleep. She thought of John. How

160

clearly she could see him with her eyes closed. The tanned, handsome face, the darkness of his eyes. She could see him clothed, unclothed, equally handsome both ways. She smiled, thinking of the sunburn he had gotten the day after their marriage. It had been the only day he had gone without clothes. "Hell, I would never make a good nudist," he had remarked that evening when she applied the after-tan lotion to his red rear. Her smile widened. He was wonderful.

She wondered what entry he had made in his log the day they had exchanged vows at sunrise. She wondered about all the entries he had made concerning her. Her eyes cut again to the book. He had told her the log kept a complete story of a voyage, entries from beginning day to final day. Everything of any and all importance was documented. At some point every day since she had come on the *Beauty* she had found him writing in the ledger. Yet he had never offered to let her read a single entry, nor had he ever allowed her to make one. For some reason he had kept the log completely from her, as though it contained some great secret.

She leaned over the side of the bunk and called up to him, "John, are you all right?"

"Yes," came his loud reply. "Go to sleep."

She fell back on her pillow and closed her eyes again. The thought she was thinking made her ashamed. She was suddenly overwrought with temptation to open the *Beauty*'s logbook. She squinched her eyes together tightly, then opened them, and sat up on the side of the bed. Slowly she pulled back the sheet and moved across the room to John's dressing table. She would tell him about it tomorrow. He would probably laugh and call her nosy female or something similiar. She picked up the cover and opened the logbook to the first page.

In that instant a loud rumbling sound like a huge clap of thunder roared in her ears, and without further warning she found herself thrown across the floor as the *Beauty* keeled sharply. Scrambling to her feet she screamed, "John!" She ran for the stairs.

His hand met her in the entrance and pushed her backward. "For God's sake, stay down there!" As he spoke a wave blacker than the blackest night towered above their heads and covered the *Beauty* like a black wall falling.

"It's a freighter!" John yelled. "It's run us down!"

The mast swung around and the sound of it scraping the steel side of the large ship filled the night. John's arms were around her tight and she clutched fervently at him. In the next seconds they stood motionless in each other's embrace, waiting to hear the fiber glass hull of the *Beauty* cracking like an egg dropped on concrete. The *Beauty* rolled in the water from rail to rail, and after a moment John exhaled a long breath of air. He began to release her, and she stood against the wall sobbing from fright. "Oh, John," she cried. "Is it over?"

He exhaled again. "I think so. The bow wave of the freighter must have thrown us far enough to avoid a full collision. I know we've got mainsail damage, but there's no way to tell how bad in this fog. We'll just have to wait until it clears."

She managed to free her voice of some of the fright. "How could this happen? With all this water around us, how could a boat run us down like that?"

"The fog," he replied knowingly. "No one on the bridge of that freighter could have seen our lights."

"But how can two ships collide in this big ocean?" She shook her head wildly with disbelief.

He tried to make his voice light. "Darling, the sky is much larger than the ocean, so how do planes manage to collide with all that space around them? I'm sure this was partly my fault. I was trying to raise Fanning on the radio instead of sending out our position to any ships in the area. I guess I wasn't thinking."

She stared at him, barely able to see his face. "Can I stay here with you?" she asked. "It's lonely in the cabin."

"I'd rather you didn't. I'll be tied up with the radio until the weather clears, and I don't want to be worried about you getting swept overboard. You can't prepare for what you can't see. I'd feel better knowing you're in the cabin." He leaned forward and kissed her lips swiftly.

She was silent. He was probably right, but she hated going back down to the cabin alone. She blinked hard. "I'll go," she said in a low voice. "I suppose I can read for a while; it might make the night pass quicker."

"Good idea." He readily agreed. "I'll check on you when I can." He kissed her again and when she turned to the steps, he patted her on the rear. "Don't worry. Everything's fine now. It was a close call, but it wasn't our first, and it probably won't be our last. Close calls come with the territory."

She clung to the stair rail a second longer, then went down. Once inside the cabin she looked again to the log. She hung back a moment, but she couldn't fully talk herself out of it. She walked to his dresser, picked up the book, and carried it under her arm to her bunk. She placed it on the bunk while she slipped off the safety harness and life jacket and pulled off the wet clothes. She put on a nightgown, her robe, and then the harness. She looked at her watch. It was only eleven thirty. It would be a long night.

Resting against the propped-up pillow, Kenda pulled her knees up and rested the book on them. She turned the pages. Nothing posted except times, dates, locations, and distances traveled. She scanned the entries, page after page. In the left column beside the date he had frequently made entries of unusual occurrences. During the first months of his voyage he had called Lillian while harbored in any port having telephone connections to the States—entries that aroused a tight sensation in her chest. One particular notation stated: "Lillian and I are making progress. Two thousand miles between us seem to aid our mutual understanding of each other." A tinge of jealousy stirred. She turned more pages. Finally she came upon the entry made the day he sailed into the lagoon of her island. A single line stated: "Found a beautiful, wild creature today marooned on island for past seven years." Kenda felt her face redden in an upsurge of fury. *Creature.* He had called her a creature.

Her eyes began to scan the columns faster. With open-mouthed disbelief she read the next entry concerning herself. "Her name is Kenda Vaughn. She has just won my contest for Miss Body Beautiful. I think the coming days will be pleasurable beyond my wildest imagination."

Kenda turned the page and at the top was the next entry made in Suva, a hastily scratched note about the call to Lillian: "We have our problems solved and at last a happy future looms on the horizon for both of us. Am anxious to return home and begin a new life." Kenda tilted her head in disbelief. "Begin a new life." With Lillian? While he had written of her as a creature, an object of pleasure, he had written of beginning a new life with—Lillian.

Now her hands moved very slowly, turning the pages in slow motion. Many entries were made about the storm. Not another single one referred to her. He must have changed his mind. At some point he must have! Still, her heart began sinking lower with each turn of the page. She moved to the entries referring to the doldrums. One simply stated: "Water, water everywhere and all the boards did shrink." She remembered the line from *The Ancient Mariner*, ninth-grade literature.

She gave a shiver as she read what was written on the day of their marriage. Nothing but the ship's location. Not a word relating to the sunrise exchange of vows, not even was her name recorded but that one time anywhere else in the entire book.

As if to escape the terrible thoughts, she slammed the book closed and slung it across the room. Angrily she blinked back the sting of tears. She would have died then if only her heart would have stopped beating. No pain had ever gripped her so. John had deceived her. John had terribly deceived her!

According to the captain's daily log record of the good ship *Beauty*, Kenda Vaughn Taylor did not exist. Kenda Vaughn did exist. She existed in that entry that referred to her as a creature and in the entry that named her pleasurable. Creatures were animals. Nothing lay idle in her mind now. *You aren't a creature, Kenda Vaughn, you're a fool, an object of pleasure. You have been, haven't you? You have certainly made the trip home to Lillian much more pleasurable for him.*

She could see him standing behind her after coming on

shore from the lagoon—his surprised expression, his broad shoulders, his flagrant masculinity. She closed her eyes. He had found a creature to tame. Remembering the strength of his arms, the thrill of his touch, she knew he had indeed tamed that creature. But no longer.

She opened her eyes and glared at the book on the floor, and she knew the wild creature was back.

CHAPTER THIRTEEN

The fog had gone and the morning light shone down on Fanning Island. During the remainder of the night Kenda had drifted into a dark mood, a state of mind in which she had never before dwelled. John had come to the cabin twice, and each time when she heard his footsteps on the stairs she had turned her face to the wall and feigned sleep.

In the morning she rose from bed like a zombie, bathed and dressed in her casual beige slacks and white blouse. She tensed when she heard John coming to the room. She could feel her insides shrinking.

He greeted her with a smile. "Good morning, sleepy-head. We've got a beautiful day out there. I've got the sails hoisted again."

She was silent.

He leaned forward to kiss her and she drew back. "Don't," she pleaded in a whisper.

"Now, is that any way to greet your husband first thing

in the morning?" His mouth brushed her cool, unresponsive lips. He straightened and looked at her, his eyes glinting with concern. "What is it?"

"John, I want to fly on to Honolu: ," she said in flat, dry words. "Do you think it can be arranged from Fanning?" She lowered her gaze from his face and looked down at the sandals on her feet.

He pulled a cigarette from his sweater pocket and lit it. "Is it the fog?" he asked, studying the red glow on the end of his cigarette. "Are you tired of sailing, or frightened? Is that it, Kenda?"

Her glance flew back to him. She looked at the lean strength in the hand holding the cigarette. What did it matter now if she told the truth or a lie? She finally nodded. "Yes, I'm tired of sailing."

He gave a ghost of a laugh. "And here you are, the woman who said she would sail the pants off me before we reached Hawaii." He raised his brows at her. "You are that woman, aren't you?"

She paused. *No*, she wanted to scream. That woman loved you, trusted you, believed in you. But she could not bring herself to utter a word.

He reached out and she felt the fingers of his left hand warm on her shoulders. His eyes were fixed on her face. "Kenda, what's going on in your mind? Won't you tell me?"

She caught her breath and wrenched herself from his touch. She bit her lip, knowing that right now, this very minute, she had to put a distance between them. He had all the years of experience with women; he knew how to handle them, how to take a woman and fill her with desire until she only wanted to fall into the trap of his arms. She

168

had to escape his eyes before he looked past the bewilderment in them and found the passion. She cut her eyes wildly down to the floor. "Can you arrange for me to fly to Hawaii, John?" she asked again, her voice sounding loud and uncontrolled. "I want to know, can you?" She tried to conceal her shaking as she moved toward the door. Once out of his reach, she looked back at him.

"Yes," he said in cold, sure words. "I can arrange it."

"Thank you." She fled out on deck. Trembling uncontrollably now, she choked back the sobs in her throat and blinked wildly to fight away the burning tears. She clutched the rail and took several deep breaths of the tangy morning air. She shivered as she saw the island etched like a green-topped mountain rising from the sea against the cloudless sky. Yesterday it would have looked so beautiful and unreal, like a wonderland for fairy-tale lovers. She braced herself, staring helplessly across the water, when she heard him come up behind her in quick long strides that brought him to beside her.

Again he questioned, "Kenda, darling, this is crazy. What is it? Won't you tell me?"

She shook her head. "There's nothing to tell." She swallowed painfully hard.

His eyes were hawklike as they fell on her face. "Don't treat me like I'm some kind of idiot. If you don't love me, tell me plain out. If you don't want to be married to me, tell me, Kenda." His voice was deep and husky. "I won't cry or beg you to stay with me. Darling, if that's it, I'll let you go. But tell me."

She forced herself to meet his eyes. Then, as all the days together seemed to start spinning around in her head, she clutched the railing again and looked at the island. Despite last night, despite what she had read in the log, or didn't read . . .

John took her chin in his hand and forced her to look at him. "That's it, isn't it? You've realized that you don't love me, that it was nice while it lasted, but it just didn't last." His breath was coming more quickly, along with his words. "You want what's out there." He pointed savagely to the island. "And beyond that island. You want the world that's going to open up to you the moment you set down in Honolulu—the bright lights, the attention, the glitter." His voice dropped lower and he brought his face closer to hers. "Well, my darling, I'm going to see that you get it, with all the trimmings!" He frowned in her face. "And if you find yourself stranded on a different kind of island, don't look for me to rescue you, lady. Rescuing you is too damned hard on the heart." He turned on his heel and disappeared below deck.

"John," she called after him, but he did not hear.

Twice through the remainder of the day she tried to work up the courage to talk to him, but each time he avoided the conversations. He remained stone-faced at the helm, his hands gripping the wheel tightly. The only words exchanged when he came to her room after dinner were those instructing her in firm, explicit tones that the helicopter from Christmas Island would arrive in the morning and carry her back to where she would have a chartered flight to Hawaii.

She had looked at him then through a blur of tears, but he had slammed in and out of her door so quickly he had not noticed.

How forlorn she felt that night in the bungalow room of his friend's house on Fanning Island. Under different circumstances the visit would have been beautiful. Few visitors stopped by the island, so they had been given the royal tour by Herbert Lansing, John's friend from his last voyage in the Pacific. In almost total silence they had witnessed the harvesting of the crop of coconuts that produced the copra that made the oil for commercial use. From there they visited the school, the village, and then back to the bungalow. Herbert's wife, Diane, had prepared a wonderful dinner which Kenda tried to wash down unsuccessfully with three glasses of red wine.

Finally, feeling strangely disjointed, she excused herself from the table and retired to her room. There she huddled on the bed, her hands clenched tight, her mind in total upheaval. John had not introduced her as his wife. How strange it all was. He had accused her of not loving him. Of not loving him.

How hard it was to keep from running to him, to keep from fleeing down the hall that separated their rooms and throwing herself in his arms. She felt empty and sad. She crouched on the large double bed and listened to the sounds of the night coming through the window.

She expected him to come for her the next morning and was surprised when she opened the door and found Herbert Lansing standing in the hallway. She felt this morning she and John might talk and smooth out the problems that had suddenly blown their love off course. After thinking about it all night, the strange entries in the logbook had lost some of their importance. Perhaps there was a logical explanation. At any rate, she wanted to hear whatever explanation did exist.

Herbert smiled at her. "John asked me to see that you got to Christmas Island safely. I'll go with you, and when you're on the way to Hawaii, the helicopter will bring me back."

Her mouth fell open. "Where is John?"

"He sailed this morning." Herbert scratched his head. "Before daybreak. Diane offered to cook, but she couldn't get him to eat a bite of breakfast."

Her hands flew to her mouth. Then she closed her eyes and fell back against the wall. The sudden pain in her heart made breathing almost impossible.

"Are you ready, Miss Vaughn?" Herbert asked. "The helicopter should land soon." He walked into the room and looked around. "Your bags?"

Still pressed hard against the wall, Kenda pointed at the foot of the bed where her packed bags waited. She watched Herbert lift the luggage from the floor and walk out of the room. It seemed forever before she could make her weak legs move so that she could follow him down the hall. She was shocked beyond feeling. John had left her. She brushed at her eyes. He had sailed away on the *Beauty* and left her, left her with a feeling of anguish she knew she would carry with her always.

Herbert Lansing made good his promise to John. Seated on the chartered jet that would fly her to Honolulu, Kenda waved at him standing at the gate. A few minutes later she was thousands of feet above the sea, and every now and then she could see a patch of aqua-blue water break into view beneath the clouds. A small group of people were on the plane with her. The pilot, co-pilot, and stewardess had greeted her warmly as had the others, but she couldn't remember any of their names, or what they said.

She could get no relief from the pain in her heart.

Though she was slicing through the air with great speed, her world stood completely still. John had sailed off without even a good-bye, and left her the loneliest person on earth. Sweet memories of the time spent with him began to tear at her unmercifully and she laid her head back against the seat and closed her eyes. The numbing realization that he had not loved her after all, had misled her, had not really made her his wife, began to surface. Exhausted from lack of sleep the past two nights, she felt her lids growing heavy. She'd loved him so much it had blinded her to reality. Her heart sank deeper and she drifted into a wave of unconsciousness.

Several hours later she felt a gentle hand on her shoulder. Slowly she opened her eyes to see the attendant smiling down at her.

"Miss Vaughn," she said softly, "I have just carried fresh coffee to the pilots, would you like a cup?"

Swallowing, Kenda nodded. A moment later, with shaking hands, she accepted the cup of hot coffee from the young woman who slid into the seat next to her. "Do you mind if I join you for a few minutes?"

"No," Kenda whispered. "Please do."

"We'll be landing in another few hours and I didn't want the entire flight to pass without talking with you." She paused. "Is it true you were marooned on an island for seven years?"

Kenda nodded. "Yes, almost seven." Suddenly a sharp homesickness for her island stabbed through her and she could feel the burning behind her eyes. She swallowed hard and sipped a long slow drink of coffee, fighting for time to overpower the emerging tears.

"Goodness, did you ever get sick or anything being

there by yourself? I would have been scared out of my mind." The young woman shook her head. "I don't know how you did it."

Kenda took another sip. "I was healthy, afraid in the beginning, but after a while the fear left."

"The man who found you, I'll bet he was surprised." She laughed low.

Kenda didn't reply for a long moment, then she whispered, "Yes, he was surprised."

"Who was he?"

"John—John Taylor from Los Angeles."

"How did he happen to find you?"

Kenda wondered if she could find the strength to answer that question. John had said fate. Fate had led him to her. Finally, she shook her head. "I—I don't know. One day I looked up and there he was." God, she felt so helpless without him now. She answered a few more questions, not even listening to her own words. She felt so tired, so weary, so alone. She felt like the whole world had rolled out from under her and left her floating in some kind of dark void. She remained that way for the rest of the night.

By morning, as the plane sped swiftly toward its destination, Kenda turned her full attention to the clear blue outside her window. Everyone on the plane with her was making preparations for the arrival in Honolulu later in the day.

Nervously she smoothed back her long blond hair, trying to replace strands that had strayed during the night. Below, somewhere in the water between Fanning and Hawaii, she knew that the *Beauty* glided smoothly. She could close her eyes and hear the sound of the water lapping against the hull. The sun had risen full and the turquoise-blue ocean was flecked with gold. She wanted to be down there on deck with John, standing at the helm with him, in the stern at the tiller, in the cabin lying beside him on the narrow bed, feeling the *Beauty* rolling gracefully amid the gentle swells.

How could this have happened? How could she suddenly find herself flying thousands of feet above the sea alone, without John? As the coast of Hawaii broke into her view, she felt that her eyes were fastened on the end of the world—not the beginning. She would soon be home. After all these years and miles, there before her stretched home. But she could not bring herself to smile. There would be no one there to greet her. This awareness filled her with an almost unbearable sadness. She was going home alone.

Why had he wanted to marry her? She had never once pushed the subject of marriage. Not once had the word marriage crossed her lips. She knew that he didn't have to marry her, not to have her love him, if that had been his reason. As he had so aptly put it, it would only have been a matter of time before the passion each fought to keep in check broke free and devoured them the way it had the day of their marriage. She lay back against the seat again and stared into the space directly in front of her eyes. She wondered if she would ever be able to smile again.

She had been mistaken to believe that no one would be on hand to meet her at the Honolulu airport. The reception she received was wild, and by the time she was put into the limousine and rushed to the hotel, she had deteriorated into a complete wreck. The questions hurled at her by the newsmen, all speaking at the same time, all trying

175

to get right in her face with their microphones, had filled her with an anxiety she couldn't hide. After what seemed like an eternity, the man from the Institute of Marine Biology had taken her arm and led her from the crowd. He had hastily opened the door of the limousine and she had slid across the seat and immediately buried her face in her hands.

"Kenda"—his voice was kind and understanding—"I tried to avoid this. We wanted to keep your arrival under wraps, but somehow word leaked out. I'm awfully sorry."

She nodded, her hands still clutching her face.

He talked on. "We met once, many years ago in San Diego. Do you remember your father being guest speaker at a seminar? He brought you along and you spent the night with my daughter, Nancy."

On the verge of tears, she looked over at him. Finally she nodded. "Yes," she whispered, "I remember." His name was William Palmer, her father had called him Bill.

"We have taken the liberty of reserving a suite for you at the Hilton." He inhaled. "Now that your father's estate can be probated, it should only be temporary. We have attorneys to look out for your interests. You don't mind, do you?"

"No. I need all the help I can get . . ." Her words drifted away. But she needed her help from John. From John, not from strangers. She needed John.

"Understandably, I suppose you have some bitterness at us for leaving you in your predicament." He spoke with quiet concern. "I speak for everyone when I say that we can't tell you how sorry we are that this happened. When we learned of your being alive several weeks ago, we were horrified to hear that you had spent all those years alone on that island. No words can convey our feelings, or our guilt."

"It wasn't your fault," Kenda replied softly. "It wasn't anyone's fault." As she spoke to him, in her own mind she knew it had been fate that left her there, not the fault of any man.

He reached over and patted her hand. It was a comforting gesture and she managed a weak smile for him.

The next days were spent with telephone calls from the mainland, visits at all hours of the day and night from various news, magazine, and television reporters, and appointments with attorneys. It seemed that slowly the door was closing on the past years as she found herself being hurled into the present with a fierceness that kept her off balance half the time. But it didn't seem natural. Nothing seemed real. Without John it was all meaningless.

On the third day, Leah, the housekeeper who had worked for them before she went to spend that fateful summer with her father, came to see her. The meeting had been joyous. Leah had brought with her a picnic basket of food and a thermos of fresh-brewed coffee.

After the hugging and crying was over, Leah started preparing the table with the various foods she had brought —sandwiches, chicken, rolls, cakes. "When I saw your picture on television last night, I made my brother get up out of his bed and bring me back to Honolulu. I said that child is so thin a good wind will blow her away."

"It looks delicious, Leah, but honestly, I don't know if I can eat a bite. My appetite has completely left me. I haven't been able to eat in days."

"Well, you are fixing to eat now, young lady. Then

177

we're going to pack your things and go home. All these people have worried you so, you look like a skeleton running around here. And I'm not going to have it. Your daddy would turn over in his grave if he knew about all this. Now, you get over here and eat."

Kenda smiled and sat down at the table by the window. She watched as Leah took the chair across from her. She picked up a sandwich and took a bite. Leah watched.

"How does it taste?"

"Delicious," Kenda lied. Every bite of food she had placed in her mouth since her last meal with John had tasted like cotton. As she chewed, she tried to work in a fleeting smile at Leah. The woman hadn't changed much in the seven years, Kenda observed. Maybe she had put on another pound or two on her already fleshy body, but the eyes, the facial expression, were still the same.

Oh, but she had changed and she wondered if Leah could see, outside of her being older, how much change had taken place over the years. Apparently Leah did, for she asked, "Are you not happy to be home, honey?"

Kenda felt a burning in her throat, almost like it was closing. She choked painfully on the bite of food she tried to swallow as she heard Leah's question. John Taylor had seduced more than her body; he had taken her mind and her emotions along with her love. He had allowed her to live a beautiful fantasy, then suddenly dumped her into reality, and now while she struggled to survive, he stood tall in the shadows of her mind, his image never leaving her even for a moment. Was she not happy to be home? That was Leah's question. How did someone answer such a question, someone who was torn between two worlds. She realized her body was in Honolulu, but her heart was somewhere out on the Pacific Ocean on a thirty-six-foot ketch with the man she married. Suddenly she knew that was where she wanted to be, had to be, needed to be. Nothing in the world mattered more than John Taylor.

She began to talk to Leah, really talk to her. She told her about John, about the voyage, about the marriage, about the events that led to their separation. While she talked Leah watched her, not interrupting, and when she finished and lapsed into silence, Leah inhaled a deep breath and asked, "Do you believe he loved you, Kenda?"

Kenda nodded tearfully. "Yes, he loved me. In spite of what he wrote in his stupid logbook, I know he loved me."

Then Leah pointed to the laden table. "Eat. If he loved you, he'll come to you. If he didn't, you've still got to live. Life goes on, honey. You, better than anyone, should know that to be the truth."

The days passed. As soon as all the legal matters were cleared, Kenda found herself to be financially well off. She purchased a small cottage for herself and Leah with a beautiful view of the ocean. She received offers from everywhere in the world to publicize the past seven years of her life—every kind of offer imaginable. She couldn't bring herself to accept any of them.

She wondered how John was spending his time. Enough days had passed that if he had planned to stop by Honolulu he would have done so. Enough days had passed for him to be home in California. She could never bring herself to call him, no matter how badly her ache for him grew. He had rejected her. She could visualize him with Lillian. He had, after all, written he was anxious to get home. Well, by now he was home.

CHAPTER FOURTEEN

And so, for some weeks, life for Kenda Vaughn Taylor went on very subdued and uneventful. There were still the daily calls that would have allowed her to capitalize on her isolated years, but she could not bring herself to do so. She hardly needed the money offered.

She passed the entrance examinations to the University of Hawaii at Honolulu and enrolled in several courses. Many young men in her classes had asked her to go out, but she refused. In her heart she was still married to John Taylor. John. Every time she thought of him, her heart lurched painfully, even with all the time that had passed. She still loved him, and time and distance could not alter that fact. Her heart never ceased to ache for him.

She would study during the day, sometimes taking her books to the beach, then attend classes four or five days a week. She could not visualize her future. Life had become a tidal wave, and wherever it swept her, she went.

She felt sure John and Lillian were together, and he would never know what that thought did to her. It seemed that all peace, happiness, and thoughts of the future had been washed completely from her life. She found herself becoming more and more dependent on Leah. She relied on Leah, yet Leah became her sternest critic.

There came a weekend when she sensed something different about the housekeeper. An entire morning went by without a lecture from the woman. Leah was happy, working busily, and all the while humming "Hawaiian Wedding Song" under her breath.

As Kenda gathered her books under her arm and prepared to go down to the beach, she eyed Leah quizzically. "Why are you so happy this morning, if I might ask?"

"It's a beautiful day." Leah lifted her brows, smiling happily. "I love beautiful days."

"Most days in Hawaii are beautiful," Kenda reminded her.

"Some more so than others," Leah replied, then went back to her dusting and humming.

Shaking her head, Kenda closed the door behind her and walked down the path to the sunny beach. She swam and played awhile in the surf, then settled down on her blanket and picked up a book. She began to read, a grim, determined expression firmly planted on her face.

"Is it really that interesting?" a voice behind her asked.

She froze. Not even a breath emerged. Not a blink of the eye. Then slowly she turned her head and looked at him.

"Hi." John smiled.

"Hi," she whispered after an eternal moment passed.

"Mind if I join you?"

She moved over on the blanket. For a moment she thought her heart would burst. He looked at her without speaking. Silently her eyes traveled over every inch of his face as if she were memorizing every detail over again.

At last he spoke: "I've missed you—very much."

She gave a little cry. "Oh, John, it's all my fault. I know it is."

Immediately he contradicted her, "No, it isn't. I know I failed you, Kenda. I don't know how. I've spent these past months racking my brain trying to figure out what I did wrong, and I don't know till this day what it was I did. Would you tell me?"

She was silent as he went on.

"I thought if I gave myself time I would come up with the answer, but I haven't been able to. It's all still a mystery to me. Please tell me, then I'll go away and leave you alone, but I've got to know. For my own peace of mind, do you understand?"

"John, you must believe me, it's all my fault. I realize that now," she said with certainty. "It was your log, the *Beauty*'s logbook. I read it the night of the fog."

He stared at her as if he didn't believe her. Then his face took on a queer, vacant look. He shook his head. "I don't understand. There was, and is, nothing in the records of the voyage that should have upset you, Kenda. I was very careful not to record about us in the log. I kept a log of us, but it was a separate journal. Is that why you're angry? Did you find the journal?" Again he shook his head. "I'm confused. I'm sorry."

She looked imploringly at him. "No, I didn't know about any journal. All I saw was the log you kept on your dresser. You only referred to me a couple of times in it and

183

then you called me a wild creature, body beautiful, pleasurable. I read the comments you'd made about Lillian, about how you two had your problems solved, how you'd be anxious to return home, how a happy future loomed for you both on the horizon, so I put two and two together and—"

"You came up with five." Suddenly he smiled and reached for her. "I should have known that anyone stranded on an island all those years couldn't possibly be expected to add correctly. You silly goose. Lillian and I had a happy future ahead because we were finished, free of each other. If you weren't so beautiful, and if I didn't love you so much, I swear I'd be tempted to turn you over my knee and tan your hide." He shook his head in disbelief. "When I think of all the time we've wasted. When I think . . ."

Her fingers touched his lips and silenced him. "Don't think," she whispered. The hunger for his touch was almost more than she could stand. She wanted so badly for him to hold her. A new wild hope had overtaken her and with a sudden groan she lifted her lips to meet his. He kissed her then released her quickly.

They stared into each other's eyes for a moment or two before slowly, haltingly, John lowered his mouth to hers again. The gentle kiss turned into a passionate demanding one. Kenda clung to him, aware of the awakened fires in her, the hunger that overpowered her, the ache for him that had been so long hidden and guarded in her heart. They were again in the world alone—nothing else existed but the two of them. Waves of pleasure rippled throughout her body, one after another.

"Hey . . . hey," he muttered, the words tumbling from

his mouth. "We aren't exactly alone here. This is not the *Beauty.*" Slowly he released her and straightened, clearing his throat.

Her breath had left her, and now she gasped to reclaim it. "Where is the *Beauty?*" she finally spoke.

"At home. I flew here this morning. I just couldn't stand it any longer. I had to come."

Kenda smiled. "Did you by any chance talk to Leah?"

He nodded. "Yes, from the airport. She gave me directions to get here." He gazed at her a long moment before saying, "Kenda, would you like to marry me again, this time a traditional marriage, with a preacher, and a reception, and a three-tiered wedding cake with a little bride and groom standing on top?"

She didn't have to think about her answer. "Yes." She sighed in a soft, trembling voice. "If that's what you want. I want whatever you want, John."

His eyes sparkled. "Of course, for me nothing will ever replace the sunrise ceremony that took place out there." He pointed to the ocean, and a faraway look filled his eyes as he whispered, bending close to her, "But you used up all the film when we sailed away from the island, so we don't have any pictures of our wedding day. We'll do it all over again." His arms tightened around her. "I love you, Kenda Vaughn Taylor. I want to spend every day for the rest of my life with you."

One week later a wedding ceremony took place in Honolulu, Hawaii. The public and press were invited. And when they were pronounced man and wife for all the world to see and hear, the two looked at each other and then they smiled.

Kenda knew as she reached out for John, and felt his arms enfold her, that she was seeing him, not in the tuxedo and ruffled shirt, but in shorts and a cotton shirt with a red bandanna tied around his hair and the sunrise reflecting golden in the still, blue waters that surrounded them. And from his smiling eyes, she knew that was the picture he, too, was seeing. That was the precious picture only they could share—the two of them alone on the *Beauty* at sunrise in the Pacific Ocean. God was their witness then— and God was their witness now.

LOOK FOR NEXT MONTH'S
CANDLELIGHT ECSTASY ROMANCES™:

84   LOVE HAS NO MERCY, *Eleanor Woods*
85   LILAC AWAKENING, *Bonnie Drake*
86   LOVE TRAP, *Barbara Andrews*
87   MORNING ALWAYS COMES, *Donna Vitek*
88   FOREVER EDEN, *Noelle Berry McCue*
89   A WILD AND TENDER MAGIC, *Rose Marie Ferris*